UNCLE SAM'S EMANCIPATION;

EARTHLY CARE,

A HEAVENLY DISCIPLINE;

AND

OTHER SKETCHES.

BY

MRS. HARRIET BEECHER STOWE,

AUTHOR OF "UNCLE TOM'S CABIN," "THE MAYFLOWER," &c.

With a Sketch of Mrs. Stowe's Family.

WILLIS P. HAZARD, 178 CHESTNUT ST.,

PHILADELPHIA.

1853.

Republished by
Negro History Press – P. O. Box 5129 – Detroit, Michigan 48236

Standard Book Number 403-00147-1

Library of Congress Catalog Card Number: 76-92442

Original copy borrowed from Oberlin College

This edition is printed on a high-quality,
acid-free paper that meets specification
requirements for fine book paper referred
to as "300-year" paper

Contents.

Account of Mrs. Beecher Stowe and her Family.

BY AN ALABAMA MAN.

THE family to which Mrs. Stowe belongs, is more widely and favourably known than almost any other in the United States. It consists of the following persons:

1. Rev. Lyman Beecher, the father, Doctor of Divinity, ex-President of Lane Theological Seminary, and late pastor of a Presbyterian Church at Cincinnati, Ohio.

2. Rev. William Beecher, pastor at Chilicothe, Ohio.

3. Rev. Edward Beecher, pastor at Boston, Massachusetts.

4. Rev. Henry Ward Beecher, pastor at Brooklyn, Long Island.

5. Rev. Charles Beecher, pastor at Newark, New Jersey.

6. Rev. Thomas Beecher, pastor at Williamsburg, New Jersey.

7. Rev. George Beecher, deceased several years since. His death was caused by the accidental discharge of a gun. At the time he was one of the most eminent men in the Western Church.

8. Mr. James Beecher, engaged in commercial business at Boston.

9. Miss Catharine Beecher.

10. Mrs. Harriet B. Stowe.

11. Mrs. Perkins.

12. Mrs. Hooker.

Twelve! the apostolic number. And of the twelve, seven apostles of the pulpit, and two of the pen, after the manner of the nineteenth century. Of the other three, one has been swept into commerce by the strong current setting that way in America; and the other two, wives of lawyers of respectable standing, and mothers of families, have been absorbed by the care and affections of domestic life. They are said to be no way inferior, in point of natural endowments, to the nine who have chosen to play their parts in life before a larger public. Indeed, persons who know intimately all the twelve, are puzzled to assign superiority to any one of them. With the shades of difference which always obtain between individual characters, they bear a striking resemblance to each other, not only physically, but intellectually and morally. All of them are about the common size—the doctor being a trifle below it, and some of the sons a trifle above it—neither stout nor slight, but compactly and ruggedly built. Their movements and gestures have much of the abruptness and want of grace common in Yankee land, where the opera and dancing school are considered as institutions of Satan. Their features are large and irregular, and though not free from a certain manly beauty in the men, are scarcely redeemed from homeliness in the women by the expression of intelligence and wit which lights them up, and fairly sparkles in their bluish gray eyes.

All of them have the energy of character, restless activity, strong convictions, tenacity of purpose, deep sympathies, and spirit of self-sacrifice, which are such invaluable qualities in the character of propagandists. It would be impossible for the theologians among them to be mem-

bers of any other church than the church militant.
Father and sons, they have been in the thickest
of the battles fought in the church and by it;
and always have moved together in solid column.
To them questions of scholastic theology are
mummeries, dry and attractionless; they are practical, living in the real present, dealing with questions which palpitate with vitality. Temperance,
foreign and home-missions, the influence of commerce on public morality, the conversion of young
men, the establishment of theological seminaries,
education, colonization, abolition, the political
obligations of Christians; on matters such as
these do the Beechers expend their energies.
Nor do they disdain taking an active part in public affairs; one of them was appointed at New
York City to address Kossuth on his arrival.
What is remarkable is that, though they have
come in violent collision with many of the abuses
of American society, their motives have never
been seriously attacked. This exemption from
the ordinary lot of reformers is owing not only
to their consistent disinterestedness, but to a certain Yankee prudence, which prevents their advancing without being sure of battalions behind

them; and also to a reputation the family has acquired for eccentricity. As public speakers they are far above mediocrity; not graceful, but eloquent, with a lively scorn of the mean and perception of the comic, which overflow in pungent wit and withering satire; and sometimes, in the heat of extemporaneous speaking, in biting sarcasm. Their style of oratory would often seem, to a staid, church-going Englishman, to contrast too strongly with the usual decorum of the pulpit.

Nine of the Beechers are authors. They are known to the reading and religious public of the United States, by reviews, essays, sermons, orations, debates, and discourses on a great variety of subjects, chiefly of local or momentary interest. All of these productions are marked by vigorous thought; very few by that artistic excellence, that conformity to the laws of the ideal, which alone confer a lasting value on the creations of the brain. Many of them are controversial, or wear an aggressive air which is unmistakable. Those which are of durable interest, and of a high order of literary merit, are six temperance sermons by Dr. Beecher; a volume of practical

1 *

sermons by the same; the "Virgin and her Son," an imaginative work by Charles Beecher, with an introduction by Mrs. Stowe; some articles on Biblical literature, by Edward Beecher; "Truth stranger than Fiction," and other tales, by Miss Catharine Beecher; "Domestic Economy," by the same; "Twelve Lectures to Young Men," by Henry Ward Beecher; "An Introduction to the Works of Charlotte Elizabeth," by Mrs. Stowe, being a collection of stories originally published in the newspapers; and "Uncle Tom's Cabin." I am sorry not to be able to place in this category many letters, essays, and addresses on Education, and particularly those from the pen of Catharine Beecher. Before Mrs. Stowe's last book, her celebrity was hardly equal to her maiden sister's. Catharine had a wider reputation as an authoress, and her indefatigable activity in the cause of education had won for her very general esteem. I may add in this connection that it is to her the United States are indebted for the only extensively useful association for preparing and sending capable female teachers to the west. She had the energy and the tact to organize and put it in successful operation.

Such is the family, in the bosom of which Mrs. Stowe's character has been formed. We cannot dismiss it without pausing before the venerable figure of the father, to whom the honour of determining the bent of the children properly belongs. Dr. Lyman Beecher is now seventy-eight years old. Born before the American Revolution, he has been, until recently, actively and ably discharging duties which would be onerous to most men in the prime of life. He was the son of a New England blacksmith, and was brought up to the trade of his father. He had arrived at mature age when he quitted the anvil, and began his collegiate studies at Yale College, New Haven. Ten years later, we find him pastor of the church at Litchfield, and rising into fame as a pulpit orator. His six sermons on temperance extended his reputation through the United States; I might say through Europe, for they ran rapidly through several editions in England, and were translated into several languages on the Continent. Being now favourably known, he was called to the pastoral charge of the most influential Presbyterian Church at Boston, where he remained until 1832. In that year, a project long

entertained by that portion of the Presbyterian
Church, whose active and enlightened piety and
liberal tendencies had gained for it the name of
New School, was put into execution; the Lane
Theological and Literary Seminary was founded.
Its object being to prepare young men for the
gospel ministry, such facilities for manual labour
were offered by it, as to make it feasible for any
young man of industry to defray, by his own
exertions, a large part of the expenses of his
own education. Dr. Beecher had long been regarded as the only man competent to direct an
institution which, it was fondly hoped, would de-
monstrate the practicability of educating mind
and body at the same time, infuse new energy
into the work of domestic and foreign missions,
and revolutionize the Presbyterian church. A
large corps of learned and able professors was
selected to aid him. The Doctor removed to his
new home in the immediate neighbourhood of
Cincinnati, and remained there until 1850, and
with what success in his chief object we shall
hereafter see.

A certain eccentricity of manner and character, and sharpness of repartee, have given rise to

hundreds of amusing anecdotes respecting Dr. Beecher. Some of them paint the man.

His lively sense of the comic elements in everything, breaks out on the most unlikely occasions. One dark night, as he was driving home with his wife and Mrs. Stowe in the carriage, the whole party was upset over a bank about fifteen feet high. They had no sooner extricated themselves from the wreck, than Mrs. Beecher and Mrs. Stowe, who were unhurt, returned thanks for their providential escape. "Speak for yourselves," said the doctor, who was feeling his bruises, "I have got a good many hard bumps, any how."

In many matters he is what Miss Olivia would have called "shiftless." None of the Goldsmith family were more so. No appeal to him for charity, or a contribution to a good cause, ever goes unresponded to, so long as he has any money in his pockets. As the family income is not unlimited, this generosity is sometimes productive of inconvenience. One day his wife had given him from the common purse twenty-five or thirty dollars in bills, with particular instructions to buy a coat, of which he stood in need. He went down to the city to make the purchase, but stop-

ping on the way to a meeting in behalf of foreign
missions, the box was handed round, and in went
his little roll of bills. He forgot his coat in his
anxiety for the Sandwich Islanders.

Well do I remember the first time I heard him
preach. It was seventeen years ago. From early
childhood I had been taught to reverence the name
of the great divine and orator, and I had long
promised myself the pleasure of listening to him.
My first Sunday morning in Cincinnati found me
sitting with his congregation. The pastor was
not as punctual as the flock. Several minutes
had elapsed after the regular hour for beginning
the service, when one of the doors opened, and I
saw a hale looking old gentleman enter. As he
pulled off his hat, half a dozen papers covered
with notes of sermons fluttered down to the floor.
The hat appeared to contain a good many more.
Stooping down and picking them up deliberately, he
came scuttling down, along the aisle, with a step
so quick and resolute as rather to alarm certain
prejudices I had on the score of clerical solem-
nity. Had I met him on a parade ground, I
should have singled him out as some general in
undress, spite of the decided stoop contracted in

study; the iron-gray hair brushed stiffly towards
the back of the head; the keen, sagacious eyes,
the firm, hard lines of the brow and wrinkled
visage, and the passion and power latent about
the mouth, with its long and scornful under-lip,
bespoke a character more likely to attack than to
defend, to do than to suffer. His manner did not
change my first impression. The ceremonies pre-
liminary to the sermon were dispatched in rather
a summary way. A petition in the long prayer
was expressed so pithily I have never forgotten
it. I forget now what reprehensible intrigue our
rulers were busy in at the time, but the doctor,
after praying for the adoption of various useful
measures, alluded to their conduct in the following terms: "And, O Lord! grant we may not
despise our rulers; and grant that they may not
act so, that we can't help it." It may be doubted
whether any English Bishop has ever uttered a
similar prayer for King and Parliament. To de-
liver his sermon, the preacher stood bolt upright,
stiff as a musket. At first, he twitched off and
replaced his spectacles a dozen times in as many
minutes with a nervous motion, gesturing meanwhile with frequent pump handle strokes of his

right arm; but as he went on, his unaffected language began to glow with animation, his simple style became figurative and graphic, and flashes of irony lighted up the dark groundwork of his Puritanical reasoning. Smiles and tears chased each other over the faces of many in the audience. His peroration was one of great beauty and power. I have heard him hundreds of times since, and he has never failed to justify his claim to the title of "the old man eloquent."

Harriet Beecher was born in Litchfield, about the year 1812. After the removal of the family to Boston, she enjoyed the best educational advantages of that city. With the view of preparing herself for the business of instruction, she acquired all the ordinary accomplishments of ladies, and much of the learning usually reserved for the stronger sex. At an early age she began to aid her eldest sister, Catharine, in the management of a flourishing female school, which had been built up by the latter. When their father went West, the sisters accompanied him, and opened a similar establishment in Cincinnati.

This city is situated on the northern bank of the Ohio. The range of hills which hugs the river for hundreds of miles above, here recedes from it in a semi-circle, broken by a valley and several ravines, leaving a basin several square miles in surface. This is the site of the busy manufacturing and commercial town which, in 1832, contained less than forty thousand inhabitants, and at present contains more than one hundred and twenty thousand — a rapid increase, which must be attributed, in a great measure, to the extensive trade it carries on with the slave States. The high hill, whose point, now crowned with an observatory, overhangs the city on the east, stretches away to the east and north in a long sweep of table-land. On this is situated Lane Seminary—Mrs. Stowe's home for eighteen long years. Near the Seminary buildings, and on the public road, are certain comfortable brick residences, situated in yards green with tufted grass, and half concealed from view by accacias, locusts, rose-bushes, and vines of honeysuckle and clematis. These were occupied by Dr. Beecher, and the Professors. There are other residences more pretending in appearance, occupied by bankers, merchants and men of fortune. The little village thus formed is called **Walnut**

Hills, and is one of the prettiest in the environs of Cincinnati.

For several years after her removal to this place, Harriet Beecher continued to teach in connection with her sister. She did so until her marriage with the Rev. Calvin E. Stowe, Professor of Biblical Literature in the Seminary of which her father was President. This gentleman was already one of the most distinguished ecclesiastical *savans* in America. After graduating with honour at Bowdoin College, Maine, and taking his theological degree at Andover, he had been appointed Professor, at Dartmouth College, New Hampshire, whence he had been called to Lane Seminary. Mrs. Stowe's married life has been of that equable and sober happiness so common in the families of Yankee clergymen. It has been blessed with a numerous offspring, of whom five are still living. Mrs. Stowe has known the fatigues of watching over the sick bed, and her heart has felt that grief which eclipses all others—that of a bereaved mother. Much of her time has been devoted to the education of her children, while the ordinary household cares have devolved on a friend or distant relative, who has always resided with her. She employed her leisure in contributing occasional pieces, tales and novelettes to the magazines and newspapers. Her writings were of a high moral tone, and deservedly popular. Only a small portion of them are comprised in the volume—"The Mayflower"—already mentioned. This part of Mrs. Stowe's life spent in literary pleasures, family joys and cares, and the society of the pious and intelligent, would have been of as unalloyed happiness as mortals can expect, had it not been darkened at every instant by the baleful shadow of slavery.

The "peculiar institution" was destined to thwart the grand project in life of Mrs. Stowe's husband and father. When they relinquished their excellent positions in the East in order to build up the great Presbyterian Seminary for the Ohio and Mississippi valley, they did so with every prospect of success. Never did a literary institution start under finer auspices. The number and reputation of the professors had drawn together several hundred students from all parts of the United States; not sickly cellar-plants of boys sent by wealthy parents, but hardy and intelligent young men, most of whom, fired by the ambition of converting the world to Christ, were winning their way through privations and toil, to education and ministerial orders. They were the stuff out of which foreign missionaries and revival preachers are made. Some of them were known to the public as lecturers: Theodore D. Weld was an oratorical celebrity. For a year all went well. Lane Seminary was the pride and hope of the church. Alas for the hopes of Messrs. Beecher and Stowe! this prosperity was of short duration.

The French Revolution of 1830, the agitation in England for reform, and against colonial slavery, the fine and imprisonment by American courts of justice, of citizens who had dared to attack the slave trade carried on under the federal flag, had begun to direct the attention of a few American philanthropists to the evils of slavery. Some years before, a society had been formed for the purpose of colonizing free blacks on the coast of Africa. It had been patronized by intelligent slaveholders, who feared the contact of free blacks with their human chattels; and by feeble or ignorant persons in the North, whose consciences impelled them to act on slavery in some way, and whose prudence or ignorance of the question led them to accept the plan favoured by slaveholders. However useful to Africa the emigration to its shores of intelligent, moral, and enterprising blacks may be, it is now universally admitted that colonization, as a means of extinguishing slavery, is a drivelling absurdity. These were the views of the Abolition Convention, which met at Philadelphia in 1833, and set on foot the agitation which has since convulsed the Union.

The President of that Convention, Mr. Arthur Tappan, was one of the most liberal donors of Lane Seminary. He forwarded its address to the students; and in a few weeks afterwards the whole subject was up for discussion amongst them. At first there was little interest. But soon the fire began to burn. Many of the students had travelled or taught school in the slave States; a goodly number were sons of slaveholders, and some were owners of slaves. They had seen slavery, and had facts to relate, many of which made the blood run chill with horror. Those spread out on the pages of "Uncle Tom's Cabin," reader, and which your swelling heart and overflowing eyes would not let you read aloud, are cold in comparison. The discussion was soon ended, for all were of accord; but the meetings for the relation of facts were continued night after night and week after week. What was at first sensibility grew into enthusiasm; the feeble flame had become a conflagration. The slave owners among the students gave liberty to their slaves; the idea of going on foreign missions was scouted at, because there were heathens at home; some left their studies and collected the coloured population of Cincinnati into churches, and preached to them; others gathered the young men into evening schools, and the children into day schools, and devoted themselves to teaching them; others organized benevolent societies for aiding them, and orphan asylums for the destitute and abandoned children; and others again, left all to aid fugitive slaves on their way to Canada, or to lecture on the evils of slavery. The fanatacism was sublime; every student felt himself a Peter the hermit, and acted as if the abolition of slavery depended on his individual exertions.

At first the discussion had been encouraged by

the President and Professors; but when they saw it swallowing up everything like regular study, they thought it high time to stop. It was too late; the current was too strong to be arrested. The commercial interests of Cincinnati took the alarm—manufacturers feared the loss of their Southern trade. Public sentiment exacted the suppression of the discussion and excitement. Slaveholders came over from Kentucky, and urged the mob on to violence. For several weeks there was imminent danger that Lane Seminary, and the houses of Drs. Beecher and Stowe, would be burnt or pulled down by a drunken rabble. These must have been weeks of mortal anxiety for Harriet Beecher. The board of trustees now interfered, and allayed the excitement of the mob by forbidding all further discussion of slavery in the Seminary. To this the students responded by withdrawing *en masse*. Where hundreds had been, there was left a mere handful. Lane Seminary was deserted. For seventeen years after this, Dr. Beecher and Professor Stowe remained there, endeavouring in vain to revive its prosperity. In 1850 they returned to the Eastern States, the great project of their life defeated.

After a short stay at Bowdoin College, Maine, Professor Stowe accepted an appointment to the chair of Biblical literature in the Theological Seminary at Andover, Massachusetts, an institution which stands, to say the least, as high as any in the United States.

These events caused a painful reaction in the feelings of the Beechers. Repulsed alike by the fanaticism they had witnessed among the foes, and the brutal violence among the friends of slavery, they thought their time for action had not come, and gave no public expression of their abhorrence of slavery. They waited for the storm to subside, and the angel of truth to mirror his form in tranquil waters. For a long time they resisted all attempts to make them bow the knee to slavery, or to avow themselves abolitionists. It is to this period Mrs. Stowe alludes, when she says, in the closing chapter of her book: "For many years of her life the author avoided all reading upon, or allusion to, the subject of slavery, considering it as too painful to be inquired into, and one which advancing light and civilization would live down." The terrible and dramatic scenes which occurred in Cincinnati, between 1835 and 1847, were calculated to increase the repugnance of a lady to mingling actively in the *melee*. That city was the chief battle-ground of freedom and slavery.   Every month there was something to attract attention to the strife; either a press destroyed, or a house mobbed, or a free negro kidnapped, or a trial for freedom before the courts, or the confectionary of an English abolitionist riddled, or a public discussion, or an escape of slaves, or an armed attack on the negro quarter, or a negro school-house razed to the ground, or a slave in prison, and killing his wife and children to prevent their being sold to the South.   The abolition press, established there in 1835 by James G. Birney, whom, on account of his mildness, Miss Martineau called "the gentleman of the abolition cause," and continued by Dr. Bailey, the moderate and able editor of the *National Era*, of Washington city, in which *Uncle Tom's Cabin* first appeared in weekly numbers, was destroyed five times.   On one occasion, the Mayor dismissed at midnight the rioters, who had also pulled down the houses of some colored people, with the following pithy speech: "Well, boys, let's go home; we've done enough."   One of these

2

mobs deserves particular notice, as its victims enlisted deeply the sympathies of Mrs. Stowe. In 1840, the slave catchers, backed by the riff-raff of the population, and urged on by certain politicians and merchants, attacked the quarters in which the negroes reside. Some of the houses were battered down by cannon. For several days the city was abandoned to violence and crime. The negro quarters were pillaged and sacked; negroes who attempted to defend their property were killed, and their mutilated bodies cast into the streets; women were violated by ruffians, and some afterwards died of the injuries received; houses were burnt, and men, women, and children were abducted in the confusion, and hurried into slavery. From the brow of the hill on which she lived, Mrs. Stowe could hear the cries of the victims, the shouts of the mob, and the reports of the guns and cannon, and could see the flames of the conflagration. To more than one of the trembling fugitives she gave shelter, and wept bitter tears with them. After the fury of the mob was spent, many of the coloured people gathered together the little left them of worldly goods, and started for Canada. Hundreds passed in front of Mrs. Stowe's house. Some of them were in little wagons ; some were trudging along on foot after the household stuff; some led their children by the hand; and there were even mothers who walked on, suckling their infants, and weeping for the dead or kidnapped husband they had left behind.

This road, which ran through Walnut Hills, and within a few feet of Mrs. Stowe's door, was one of the favourite routes of " the under-ground railroad," so often alluded to in Uncle Tom's Cabin.   This name was given to a line of Quakers and other abolitionists, who, living at intervals of 10, 15 or 20 miles between the Ohio river and the Northern lakes, had formed themselves into a sort of association to aid fugitive slaves in their escape to Canada. Any fugitive was taken by night on horseback, or in covered wagons, from station to station, until he stood on free soil, and found the fold of the lion banner floating over him, and the artillery of the British empire between him and slavery. The first station north of Cincinnati was a few miles up Mill Creek, at the house of the pious and honest-hearted John Vanzandt, who figures in chapter nine of *Uncle*

Tom's Cabin, as John Van Trompe. Mrs. Stowe
must have often been roused from her sleep by
the quick rattle of the covered wagons, and the
confused galloping of the horses of constables
and slave-catchers in hot pursuit. "Honest
John" was always ready to turn out with his team,
and the hunters of men were not often adroit
enough to come up with him. He sleeps now in
the obscure grave of a martyr. The "gigantic
frame," of which the novelist speaks, was worn
down at last by want of sleep, exposure, and
anxiety; and his spirits were depressed by the
persecutions which were accumulated on him.
Several slave owners, who had lost their property
by his means, sued him in the United States
Courts for damages; and judgment after judgment stripped him of his farm, and all his property.

During her long residence on the frontier of
the slave States, Mrs. Stowe made several visits
to them. It was then, no doubt, she made the
observations which have enabled her to paint noble, generous, and humane slaveholders, in the
characters of Wilson, the manufacturer, Mrs.
Shelby and her son George, St. Clair and his
daughter Eva, the benevolent purchaser at the

New Orleans auction sale, the mistress of Susan and Emeline, and Symes, who helped Eliza and her boy up the river bank. Mrs. Stowe has observed slavery in every phase; she has seen masters and slaves at home, New Orleans markets, fugitives, free coloured people, pro-slavery politicians and priests, abolitionists, and colonizationists. She and her family have suffered from it; seventeen years of her life have been clouded by it. For that long period she stifled the strongest emotions of her heart. No one but her intimate friends knew their strength. She has given them expression at last. *Uncle Tom's Cabin* is the agonizing cry of feelings pent up for years in the heart of a true woman.

Uncle Sam's Emancipation.

A SKETCH.

IT may be gratifying to those who desire to think well of human nature, to know that the leading incidents of the subjoined sketch are literal matters of fact, occurring in the city of Cincinnati, which have come within the scope of the writer's personal knowledge—the incidents have merely been clothed in a dramatic form, to present them more vividly to the reader.

In one of the hotel parlors of our queen city, a young gentleman, apparently in no very easy frame of mind, was pacing up and down the room, looking alternately at his watch and out of the window, as if expecting somebody. At last he rang the bell violently, and a hotel servant soon appeared.

"Has my man Sam come in yet?" he inquired.

The polished yellow gentleman to whom this was addressed, answered with a polite, but somewhat sinister smirk, that nothing had been seen of him since early that morning.

"Lazy dog! full three hours since I sent him off to B—— street, and I have seen nothing of him since."

The yellow gentleman remarked with consolatory politeness, that "he hoped Sam had not *run away*," adding, with an ill-concealed grin, that "them boys was mighty apt to show the clean heel when they come into a free State."

"Oh, no; I'm quite easy as to that," returned the young gentleman; "I'll risk Sam's ever being willing to part from me. I brought him because I was sure of him."

"Don't you be too sure," remarked a gentleman from behind, who had been listening to the conversation. "There are plenty of mischief-making busybodies on the trail of every southern gentleman, to interfere with his family matters, and decoy off his servants."

"Didn't I see Sam talking at the corner with the Quaker Simmons?" said another servant, who meanwhile had entered.

"Talking with Simmons, was he?" remarked the last speaker, with irritation; "that rascal

Simmons does nothing else, I believe, but tote away gentlemen's servants. Well, if Simmons has got him, you may as well be quiet; you'll not see your fellow again in a hurry."

"And who the deuce is this Simmons?" said our young gentleman, who, though evidently of a good natured mould, was now beginning to wax wroth; "and what business has he to interfere with other people's affairs?"

"You had better have asked those questions a few days ago, and then you would have kept a closer eye on your fellow; a meddlesome, canting, Quaker rascal, that all these black hounds run to, to be helped into Canada, and nobody knows where all."

The young gentleman jerked out his watch with increasing energy, and then walking fiercely up to the coloured waiter, who was setting the dinner table with an air of provoking satisfaction, he thundered at him, "You rascal, you understand this matter; I see it in your eyes."

Our gentleman of colour bowed, and with an air of mischievous intelligence, protested that he never interfered with other gentlemen's matters, while sundry of his brethren in office looked unutterable things out of the corners of their eyes.

"There is some cursed plot hatched up among you," said the young man. "You have talked Sam into it; I know he never would have thought of leaving me unless he was put up to it. Tell me now," he resumed, "have you heard Sam say anything about it? Come, be reasonable," he added, in a milder tone, "you shall find your account in it."

Thus adjured, the waiter protested he would be happy to give the gentleman any satisfaction in his power. The fact was, Sam had been pretty full of notions lately, and had been to see Simmons, and in short, he should not wonder if he never saw any more of him.

And as hour after hour passed, the whole day, the whole night, and no Sam was forthcoming, the truth of the surmise became increasingly evident. Our young hero, Mr. Alfred B——, was a good deal provoked, and strange as the fact may seem, a good deal grieved too, for he really loved the fellow. "Loved him!" says some scornful zealot; "a slaveholder *love* his slave!" Yes, brother; why not? A warm-hearted man will love his dog, his horse, even to grieving bitterly for their loss, and why not credit the fact that such a one

2 *

may *love* the human creature whom custom has placed on the same level. The fact was, Alfred B—— did love this young man; he had been appropriated to him in childhood; and Alfred had always redressed his grievances, fought his battles, got him out of scrapes, and purchased for him, with liberal hand, indulgences to which his comrades were strangers. He had taken pride to dress him smartly, and as for hardship and want, they had never come near him.

"The poor, silly, ungrateful puppy!" soliloquized he, "what can he do with himself? Confound that Quaker, and all his meddlesome tribe— been at him with their bloody-bone stories, I suppose—Sam knows better, the scamp—halloa, there," he called to one of the waiters, "where does this Simpkins—Simon—Simmons, or what d'ye call him, live?"

"His shop is No. 5, on G. street."

"Well, I'll go at him, and see what business he has with my affairs."

The Quaker was sitting at the door of his shop, with a round, rosy, good-humoured face, so expressive of placidity and satisfaction, that it was difficult to approach in ireful feeling.

"Is your name Simmons?" demanded Alfred, in a voice whose natural urbanity was somewhat sharpened by vexation.

"Yes, friend; what dost thou wish?"

"I wish to inquire whether you have seen anything of my coloured fellow, Sam; a man of twenty-five, or thereabouts, lodging at the Pearl street House?"

"I rather suspect that I have," said the Quaker, in a quiet, meditative tone, as if thinking the matter over with himself.

"And is it true, sir, that you have encouraged and assisted him in his efforts to get out of my service?"

"Such, truly, is the fact, my friend."

Losing patience at this provoking equanimity, our young friend poured forth his sentiments with no inconsiderable energy, and in terms not the most select or pacific, all which our Quaker received with that placid, full-orbed tranquillity of countenance, which seemed to say, "Pray, sir, relieve your mind; don't be particular, scold as hard as you like." The singularity of this expression struck the young man, and as his wrath became gradually spent, he could hardly help laughing at the tranquillity of his opponent, and he gradually changed his tone for one of expostulation. "What motive could induce you, sir, thus to incommode a stranger, and one who never injured you at all?"

"I am sorry thou art incommoded," rejoined the Quaker. "Thy servant, as thee calls him, came to me, and I helped him, as I would any other poor fellow in distress."

"Poor fellow!" said Alfred, angrily; "that's the story of the whole of you. I tell you there is not a free negro in your city so well off as my Sam is, and always has been, and he'll find it out before long."

"But tell me, friend, thou mayest die as well as another man; thy establishment may fall into debt, as well as another man's; and thy Sam may be sold by the Sheriff for debt, or change hands in dividing the estate, and so, though he was bred easily, and well cared for, he may come to be a field hand, under hard masters, starved, beaten, overworked—such things do happen sometimes, do they not?"

"Sometimes, perhaps they do," replied the young man.

"Well, look you, by our laws in Ohio, thy Sam

is now a free man; as free as I or thou; he hath a strong back, good hands, good courage, can earn his ten or twelve dollars a month—or do better. Now taking all things into account, if thee were in his place, what would thee do—would thee go back a slave, or try thy luck as a free man?"

Alfred said nothing in reply to this, only after a while he murmured half to himself, "I thought the fellow had more gratitude, after all my kindness."

"Thee talks of gratitude," said the Quaker, "now how does that account stand? Thou hast fed, and clothed, and protected this man; thou hast not starved, beaten, or abused him—that would have been unworthy of thee; thou hast shown him special kindness, and in return he has given thee faithful service for fifteen or twenty years; all his time, all his strength, all he could do or be, he has given thee, and ye are about even." The young man looked thoughtful, but made no reply.

"Sir," said he at last, "I will take no unfair advantage of you; I wish to get my servant once more; can I do so?"

"Certainly. I will bring him to thy lodgings

this evening, if thee wish it. I know thee will do what is fair," said the Quaker.

It were difficult to define the thoughts of the young man, as he returned to his lodgings. Naturally generous and humane, he had never dreamed that he had rendered injustice to the human beings he claimed as his own. Injustice and oppression he had sometimes seen with detestation, in other establishments; but it had been his pride that they were excluded from his own. It had been his pride to think that his indulgence and liberality made a situation of dependence on him preferable even to liberty.

The dark picture of possible reverses which the slave system hangs over the lot of the most favoured slaves, never occurred to him. Accordingly, at six o'clock that evening, a light tap at the door of Mr. B.'s parlor, announced the Quaker, and hanging back behind him, the reluctant Sam, who, with all his newly-acquired love of liberty, felt almost as if he were treating his old master rather shabbily, in deserting him.

"So, Sam," said Alfred, "how is this? they say you want to leave me."

"Yes, master."

"Why, what's the matter, Sam? haven't I always been good to you; and has not my father always been good to you?"

"Oh yes, master; very good."

"Have you not always had good food, good clothes, and lived easy?"

"Yes, master."

"And nobody has ever abused you?"

"No, master."

"Well, then, why do you wish to leave me?"

"Oh, massa, I want to be a free man."

"Why, Sam, ain't you well enough off now?"

"Oh, massa may die; then nobody knows who get me; some dreadful folks, you know, master, might get me, as they did Jim Sanford, and nobody to take my part. No, master, I rather be free man."

Alfred turned to the window, and thought a few moments, and then said, turning about, "Well, Sam, I believe you are right. I think, on the whole, I'd like best to be a free man myself, and I must not wonder that you do. So, for ought I see, you must go; but then, Sam, there's your wife and child." Sam's countenance fell.

"Never mind, Sam. I will send them up to you."

"Oh, master!"

"I will; ut you must remember now, Sam, you have got both yourself and them to take care of, and have no master to look after you; be steady, sober, and industrious, and then if ever you get into distress, send word to me, and I'll help you." Lest any accuse us of over-colouring our story, we will close it by extracting a passage or two from the letter which the generous young man the next day left in the hands of the Quaker, for his emancipated servant. We can assure our readers that we copy from the original document, which now lies before us:

Dear Sam—I am just on the eve of my departure for Pittsburg; I may not see you again for a long time, possibly never, and I leave this letter with your friends, Messrs. A. and B., for you, and herewith bid you an affectionate farewell. Let me give you some advice, which is, now that you are a free man, in a free State, be obedient as you were when a slave; perform all the duties that are required of you, and do all you can for your own future welfare and respectability. Let me assure you that I have the same good feeling towards you that you know I always had; and let me tell you further, that if ever you want a friend, call or write to me, and I will be that friend. Should you be sick, and not able to work, and want money to a small amount at different times, write to me, and I will always let you have it. I have not with me at present much money, though I will leave with my agent here, the Messrs. W., five dollars for you; you must give them a receipt for it. On my return from Pittsburg, I will call and see you if I have time; fail not to write to my father, for he made you a good master, and you should always treat him with respect, and cherish his memory so long as you live. Be good, industrious, and honourable, and if unfortunate in your undertakings, never forget that you have a friend in me. Farewell, and believe me your affectionate young master and friend. ALFRED B———.

That dispositions as ingenuous and noble as that of this young man, are commonly to be found either in slave States or free, is more than we dare to assert. But when we see such found, even among those who are born and bred slaveholders, we cannot but feel that there is encouragement for a fair, and mild, and brotherly presentation of truth, and every reason to lament hasty and wholesale denunciations. The great error of controversy is, that it is ever ready to assail *persons* rather than *principles*. The slave *system*, as a system, perhaps concentrates more wrong than any other now existing, and yet those who live under and in it may be, as we see, enlightened, generous, and amenable to reason. If the *system* alone is attacked, such minds will be the first to perceive its evils, and to turn against it; but if the system be attacked through individuals, self-love, wounded pride, and a thousand natural feelings, will be at once enlisted for its preservation. We therefore subjoin it as the moral of our story, that a man who has had the misfortune to be born and bred a slaveholder, may be enlightened, generous, humane, and capable of the most disinterested regard to the welfare of his slave.

Earthly Care, a Heavenly Discipline.

NOTHING is more frequently felt and spoken of as a hindrance to the inward life of devotion, than the "cares of life;" and even upon the showing of our Lord himself, the cares of the world are the thorns that choke the word, and render it unfruitful.

And yet, if this is a necessary and inevitable result of worldly cares, why does the providence of God so order things that they form so large and unavoidable a part of every human experience? Why is the physical system of man framed with such daily, oft-returning wants? Why has God arranged an outward system, which is a constant diversion from the inward—a weight on its wheels—a burden on its wings—and then commanded a strict and rigid inwardness and spirituality? Why has he placed us where the things that are seen and temporal must unavoidably have so much of our thoughts, and time, and care, and yet told us, "Set your affections on things above,

and not on things on the earth;" "Love not the
world, neither the things in the world?" And
why does one of our brightest examples of Christian experience, as it should be, say, "While we
look not at the things which are seen, but at the
things which are not seen: for the things which
are seen are temporal, but the things which are
not seen are eternal?"

The Bible tells us that our whole existence here
is *disciplinary ;* that this whole physical system,
by which our spirit is connected with all the joys
and sorrows, hopes, and fears, and wants which
form a part of it, is designed as an education to
fit the soul for its immortality. Hence, as worldly
care forms the greater part of the staple of every
human life, there must be some mode of viewing
and meeting it, which converts it from an enemy
of spirituality into a means of grace and spiritual
advancement.

Why, then, do we so often hear the lamentation, "It seems to me as if I could advance to
the higher stages of Christian life, if it were not
for the pressure of my business, and the multitude
of my worldly cares?" Is it not God, O Christian! who, in his providence, has laid these cares

upon thee, and who still holds them about thee, and permits no escape from them? If God's great undivided object is thy spiritual improvement, is there not some misapprehension or wrong use of these cares, if they do not tend to advance it? Is it not even as if a scholar should say, I could advance in science were it not for all the time and care which lessons, and books, and lectures require?

How, then, shall earthly care become heavenly discipline? How shall the disposition of the weight be altered so as to press the spirit upward towards God, instead of downward and away? How shall the pillar of cloud which rises between us and Him, become one of fire, to reflect upon us constantly the light of his countenance, and to guide us over the sands of life's desert?

It appears to us that the great radical difficulty lies in a wrong belief. There is not a genuine and real belief of the presence and agency of God in the minor events and details of life, which is necessary to change them from secular cares into spiritual blessings.

It is true there is much loose talk about an overruling Providence; and yet, if fairly stated, the belief of a great many Christians might be thus expressed: God has organized and set in operation certain general laws of matter and mind, which work out the particular results of life, and over these laws he exercises a general supervision and care, so that all the great affairs of the world are carried on after the counsel of his own will: and, in a certain *general* sense, all things are working together for good to those that love God. But when some simple-minded and child-like Christian really proceeds to refer all the *smaller* events of life to God's immediate care and agency, there is a smile of incredulity—and it is thought that the good brother displays more Christian feeling than sound philosophy.

But as the life of every individual is made up of fractions and minute atoms—as those things, which go to affect habits and character, are small and hourly recurring, it comes to pass, that a belief in Providence so very wide and general is altogether inefficient for consecrating and rendering sacred the great body of what comes in contact with the mind in the experience of life. Only once in years does the Christian, with this kind of belief, hear the voice of the Lord speak-

ing to him. When the hand of death is laid on
his child, or the bolt strikes down the brother by
his side; then, indeed, he feels that God is draw-
ing near; he listens humbly for the inward voice
that shall explain the meaning and need of this
discipline. When, by some unforeseen occur-
rence, the whole of his earthly property is swept
away, and he becomes a poor man, this event, in
his eyes, assumes sufficient magnitude to have
come from God, and to have a design and meaning; but when smaller comforts are removed,
smaller losses are encountered, and the petty
every-day vexations and annoyances of life press
about him, he recognises no God, and hears no
voice, and sees no design. Hence John Newton
says, "Many Christians, who bear the loss of
a child or the destruction of all their property
with the most heroic Christian fortitude, are entirely vanquished and overcome by the breaking
of a dish, or the blunders of a servant, and show
so unchristian a spirit, that we cannot but wonder
at them."

So when the breath of slander, or the pressure
of human injustice, comes so heavily on a man,
as really to threaten loss of character, and de-

struction of his temporal interests, he seems
forced to recognise the hand and voice of God
through the veil of human agencies, and in time-
honoured words to say—

> When men of spite against me join,
> They are the sword, the hand is thine.

But the smaller injustice, and fault-finding, which
meets every one more or less in the daily inter-
course of life—the overheard remark—the implied
censure—too petty perhaps to be even spoken of—
these daily-recurring sources of disquietude and
unhappiness are not referred to God's providence,
nor considered as a part of his probation and discipline. Those thousand vexations which come
upon us through the unreasonableness, the carelessness, the various constitutional failings or ill
adaptedness of others to our peculiarities of character, from a very large item of the disquietudes
of life, and yet how very few look beyond the
human agent, and feel that these are trials coming from God. Yet it is true, in many cases, that
these so-called minor vexations form the greater
part, and, in some cases, the only discipline of
life; and to those who do not view them as indi-

vidually ordered or permitted by God, and coming upon them by design, their affliction really
" cometh of the dust," and their trouble springs
" out of the ground ;" it is sanctified and relieved
by no Divine presence and aid, but borne alone,
and in a mere human spirit, and by mere human
reliances ; it acts on the mind as a constant diversion and hindrance, instead of moral discipline.

Hence, too, arises a coldness, and generality,
and wandering of mind in prayer. The things
that are on the heart, that are distracting the
mind, that have filled the heart so full that there
is no room for anything else, are all considered
too small and undignified to come within the pale
of a prayer : and so, with a wandering mind and a
distracted heart, the Christian offers up his prayer
for things which he thinks he *ought* to want, and
makes no mention of those which he really *does*
want. He prays that God would pour out his
Spirit on the heathen, and convert the world, and
build up his kingdom everywhere, when perhaps
a whole set of little anxieties and wants and vexations are so distracting his thoughts, that he
hardly knows what he has been saying. A faith-
less servant is wasting his property, a careless or

3

blundering workman has spoiled a lot of goods, a child is vexatious or unruly, a friend has made promises and failed to keep them, an acquaintance has made unjust or satirical remarks, some new furniture has been damaged or ruined by carelessness in the household; but all this trouble forms no subject matter for prayer, though there it is all the while lying like lead on the heart, and keeping it down so that it has no power to expand and take in anything else. But were God in Christ known and regarded as the soul's familiar Friend; were every trouble of the heart, as it rises, breathed into His bosom; were it felt that there is not one of the smallest of life's troubles that has not been permitted by Him, and *permitted for specific good purpose to the soul*, how much more heart-work would there be in prayer; how constant, how daily might it become, how it might settle and clear the atmosphere of the soul, how it might so dispose and lay away many anxieties which now take up their place there, that there might be room for the higher themes and considerations of religion!

Many sensitive and fastidious natures are worn away by the constant friction of what are called little troubles. Without any great affliction, they feel that all the flower and sweetness of their life is faded; their eye grows dim, their cheek care-worn, and their spirit loses hope and elasticity, and becomes bowed with premature age; and in the midst of tangible and physical comfort, they are restless and unhappy. The constant under-current of little cares and vexations, which is slowly wearing out the finer springs of life, is seen by no one; scarcely ever do they speak of these things to their nearest friends. Yet were there a friend, of a spirit so discerning as to feel and sympathize in all these things, how much of this repressed electric restlessness would pass off through such a sympathizing mind.

Yet among human friends this is all but impos-sible, for minds are so diverse that what is a trial and a care to one, is a matter of sport and amuse-ment to another, and all the inner world breathed into a human ear, only excites a surprised or con-temptuous pity. To whom then shall the soul turn—who will *feel* that to be affliction, which each spirit *knows* to be so? If the soul shut itself within itself, it becomes morbid; the fine chords of the mind and nerves, by constant wear, become jarring and discordant: hence fretfulness, discontent, and habitual irritability steal over the sincere Christian.

But to the Christian who really believes in the agency of God in the smallest events of life, confides in his love and makes his sympathy his refuge, the thousand minute cares and perplexities of life become each one a fine affiliating bond between the soul and its God. Christ is known, not by abstract definition, and by high-raised conceptions of the soul's aspiring hours, but known as a man knoweth his friend; he is known by the hourly wants he supplies—known by every care with which he momentarily sympathises, every apprehension which relieves, every temptation which he enables us to surmount. We learn to know Christ as the infant child learns to know its mother and father, by all the helplessness and all the dependence which are incident to this commencement of our moral existence; and as we go on thus year by year, and find in every changing situation, in every reverse, in every trouble, from the lightest sorrow to those which wring our soul from its depths, that he is equally present, and that his gracious aid is equally adequate, our faith seems gradually almost to change to sight, and Christ's sympathy, his love and care, seem to us more real than any other source of reliance; and multiplied cares and trials are only new avenues of acquaintance between us and Heaven.

Suppose, in some bright vision unfolding to our view, in tranquil evening or solemn midnight, the glorified form of some departed friend should appear to us with the announcement, "This year is to be to you one of special probation and discipline, with reference to perfecting you for a heavenly state. Weigh well and consider every incident of your daily life, for not one is to fall out by accident, but each one shall be a finished and indispensable link in a bright chain that is to draw you upward to the skies."

With what new eyes should we now look on our daily lot! and if we found in it not a single change—the same old cares, the same perplexities, the same uninteresting drudgeries still—with what new meaning would every incident be invested, and with what other and sublimer spirit could we meet them! Yet, if announced by one rising from the dead with the visible glory of a spiritual world, this truth could be asserted no more clearly and distinctly than Jesus Christ has stated it already. Not a sparrow falleth to the ground without our Father—not one of them is forgotten by him; and we are of more value than many sparrows—yea, even the hairs of our head are all numbered. Not till belief in these declarations, in their most literal sense, becomes the calm and settled habit of the soul, is life ever redeemed from drudgery and dreary emptiness, and made full of interest, meaning, and Divine significance. Not till then do its grovelling wants, its wearing cares, its stinging vexations, become to us ministering spirits—each one, by a silent but certain agency, fitting us for a higher and perfect sphere.

HYMN.

NEARER, my God, to Thee,
     Nearer to Thee !
E'en though it be a cross
     That raiseth me ;
Still all my song shall be,
Nearer, my God, to Thee,
     Nearer to Thee !

Though like a wanderer,
     The sun gone down,
Darkness comes over me,
     My rest a stone,
Yet in my dreams I'd be
Nearer, my God, to Thee,—
     Nearer to Thee !

There let my way appear
     Steps unto heav'n ;
All that Thou sendest me
     In mercy giv'n ;
Angels to beckon me
Nearer, my God, to Thee,—
     Nearer to Thee !

A Scholar's Adventures in the Country.

"If we could only live in the country," said my wife, "how much easier it would be to live."

"And how much cheaper!" said I.

"To have a little place of our own, and raise our own things!" said my wife: "dear me! I am heart-sick when I think of the old place at home, and father's great garden. What peaches and melons we used to have—what green peas and corn! Now one has to buy every cent's worth of these things—and how they taste! Such wilted, miserable corn! Such peas! Then, if we lived in the country, we should have our own cow, and milk and cream in abundance—our own hens and chickens. We could have custard and ice cream every day!"

"To say nothing of the trees and flowers, and all that," said I.

The result of this little domestic duet was that my wife and I began to ride about the city of ——— to look up some pretty interesting cottage where our visions of rural bliss might be realized. Country residences near the city we found to bear rather a high price; so that it was no easy matter to find a situation suitable to the length of our purse; till, at last, a judicious friend suggested a happy expedient—

"Borrow a few hundred," he said, "and give your note—you can save enough very soon, to make the difference. When you raise everything you eat, you know it will make your salary go a wonderful deal further."

"Certainly it will," said I. "And what can be more beautiful than to buy places by the simple process of giving one's note—'tis so neat, and handy, and convenient!"

"Why," pursued my friend, "there is Mr. B., my next door neighbour—'tis enough to make one sick of life in the city to spend a week out on his farm. Such princely living as one gets; and he assures me that it costs him very little—scarce anything, perceptible, in fact!"

"Indeed," said I, "few people can say that."

"Why," said my friend, "he has a couple of peach trees for every month, from June till frost, that furnish as many peaches as he and his wife

3 *

and ten children can dispose of. And then he has grapes, apricots, &c.; and last year his wife sold fifty dollars worth from her strawberry patch, and had an abundance for the table besides.   Out of the milk of only one cow they had butter enough to sell three or four pounds a week, besides abundance of milk and cream; and madam has the butter for her pocket money.   This is the way country people manage."

"Glorious!" thought I.   And my wife and I could scarce sleep all night, for the brilliancy of our anticipations!

To be sure our delight was somewhat damped the next day by the coldness with which my good old uncle, Jeremiah Standfast, who happened along at precisely this crisis, listened to our visions.

"You'll find it *pleasant*, children, in the summer-time," said the hard-fisted old man, twirling his blue checked pocket handkerchief; "but I'm sorry you've gone in debt for the land."

"Oh! but we shall soon save that—it's so much cheaper living in the country!" said both of us together.

"Well, as to that, I don't think it is to city-bred folks."

Here I broke in with a flood of accounts of Mr. B.'s peach trees, and Mrs. B.'s strawberries, butter, apricots, &c., &c.; to which the old gentleman listened with such a long, leathery, unmoved quietude of visage as quite provoked me, and gave me the worst possible opinion of his judgment. I was disappointed too; for, as he was reckoned one of the best practical farmers in the county, I had counted on an enthusiastic sympathy with all my agricultural designs.

"I tell you what, children," he said, "a body can live in the country, as you say, amazin' cheap; but, then, a body must *know how*"—and my uncle spread his pocket handkerchief thoughtfully out upon his knees, and shook his head gravely.

I thought him a terribly slow, stupid old body, and wondered how I had always entertained so high an opinion of his sense.

"He is evidently getting old!" said I to my wife; "his judgment is not what it used to be."

At all events, our place was bought, and we moved out, well pleased, the first morning in April, not at all remembering the ill savor of that day for matters of wisdom. Our place was a pretty cottage, about two miles from the city, with

grounds that have been tastefully laid out. There
was no lack of winding paths, arbors, flower borders, and rose-bushes, with which my wife was
especially pleased. There was a little green lot,
strolling off down to a brook, with a thick grove
of trees at the end, where our cow was to be
pastured.

The first week or two went on happily enough
in getting our little new pet of a house into trim-
ness and good order; for, as it had been long for
sale, of course there was any amount of little re-
pairs that had been left to amuse the leisure
hours of the purchaser. Here a door-step had
given way, and needed replacing; there a shutter
hung loose, and wanted a hinge; abundance of
glass needed setting; and, as to the painting and
papering, there was no end to that; then my wife
wanted a door cut here, to make our bed-room
more convenient, and a china closet knocked up
there, where no china closet before had been.
We even ventured on throwing out a bay window
from our sitting-room, because we had luckily
lighted on a workman who was so cheap that it
was an actual saving of money to employ him.
And to be sure our darling little cottage did lift

up its head wonderfully for all this garnishing and furbishing. I got up early every morning, and nailed up the rose-bushes, and my wife got up and watered the geraniums, and both flattered ourselves and each other on our early hours and thrifty habits. But soon, like Adam and Eve in Paradise, we found our little domain to ask more hands than ours to get it into shape. "So," says I to my wife, "I will bring out a gardener when I come next time, and he shall lay it out, and get it into order; and after that, I can easily keep it by the work of my leisure hours."

Our gardener was a very sublime sort of a man—an Englishman, and, of course, used to laying out noblemen's places, and we became as grasshoppers in our own eyes, when he talked of Lord this and that's estate, and began to question us about our carriage-drive and conservatory, and we could with difficulty bring the gentleman down to any understanding of the humble limits of our expectations—merely to dress out the walks and lay out a kitchen garden, and plant potatoes, turnips, beets, and carrots, was quite a descent for him. In fact, so strong were his æsthetic preferences, that he persuaded my wife to let him dig all the

turf off from a green square opposite the bay window, and to lay it out into divers little triangles,
resembling small pieces of pie, together with cir-
cles, mounds, and various other geometrical ornaments, the planning and planting of which soon
engrossed my wife's whole soul.   The planting of
the potatoes, beets, carrots, &c., was intrusted to
a raw Irishman; for, as to me, to confess the
truth, I began to fear that digging did not agree
with me.   It is true that I was exceedingly vigorous at first, and actually planted with my own
hands two or three long rows of potatoes; after
which I got a turn of rheumatism in my shoulder
which lasted me a week.   Stooping down to plant
beets and radishes gave me a vertigo, so that I
was obliged to content myself with a general super-
intendence of the garden; that is to say, I charged
my Englishman to see that my Irishman did his
duty properly, and then got on to my horse and
rode to the city.   But about one part of the matter I must say I was not remiss—and that is, in
the purchase of seed and garden utensils.   Not a
day passed that I did not come home with my
pockets stuffed with choice seeds, roots, &c., and
the variety of my garden utensils was unequalled.

There was not a pruning-hook of any pattern, not a hoe, rake, or spade, great or small, that I did not have specimens of; and flower seeds and bulbs were also forthcoming in liberal proportions. In fact, I had opened an account at a thriving seed store; for when a man is driving a business on a large scale, it is not always convenient to hand out the change for every little matter, and buying things on account is as neat and agreeable a mode of acquisition as paying bills with one's note.

"You know we must have a cow," said my wife, the morning of our second week. Our friend the gardener, who had now worked with us at the rate of two dollars a day for two weeks, was at hand in a moment in our emergency. We wanted to buy a cow, and he had one to sell—a wonderful cow, of a real English breed. He would not sell her for any money, except to oblige particular friends; but as we had patronized him, we should have her for forty dollars. How much we were obliged to him! The forty dollars were speedily forthcoming, and so also was the cow.

"What makes her shake her head in that way?" said my wife, apprehensively, as she observed the interesting beast making sundry demonstrations with her horns. "I hope she's mild and gentle."

The gardener fluently demonstrated that the animal was a pattern of all the softer graces, and that this head-shaking was merely a little nervous affection consequent on the embarrassment of a new position. We had faith to believe almost anything at this time, and therefore came from the barn-yard to the house as much satisfied with our purchase as Job with his three thousand camels and five hundred yoke of oxen. Her quondam master milked her for us the first evening, out of a delicate regard to her feelings as a stranger, and we fancied that we discerned forty dollars' worth of excellence in the very quality of the milk.

But alas! the next morning our Irish girl came in with a most rueful face: "And is it milking that baste you'd have me be after?" she said; "sure, and she won't let me come near her."

"Nonsense, Biddy!" said I, "you frightened her, perhaps; the cow is perfectly gentle;" and with the pail on my arm I sallied forth. The moment madam saw me entering the cow-yard, she greeted me with a very expressive flourish of her horns.

"This won't do," said I, and I stopped. The lady evidently was serious in her intentions of resisting any personal approaches. I cut a cudgel, and putting on a bold face, marched towards her, while Biddy followed with her milking-stool. Apparently, the beast saw the necessity of temporizing, for she assumed a demure expression, and Biddy sat down to milk. I stood sentry, and if the lady shook her head, I shook my stick, and thus the milking operation proceeded with tolerable serenity and success.

"There!" said I, with dignity, when the frothing pail was full to the brim. "That will do, Biddy," and I dropped my stick. Dump! came madam's heel on the side of the pail, and it flew like a rocket into the air, while the milky flood showered plentifully over me, in a new broadcloth riding-coat that I had assumed for the first time that morning. "Whew!" said I, as soon as I could get my breath from this extraordinary shower-bath; "what's all this?" My wife came running toward the cow-yard, as I stood with the milk streaming from my hair, filling my eyes, and dropping from the tip of my nose! and she and Biddy performed a recitative lamentation over me in alternate strophes, like the chorus in a Greek tragedy. Such was our first morning's experience; but as we had announced our bargain with some considerable flourish of trumpets among our neighbours and friends, we concluded to hush the matter up as much as possible.

"These very superior cows are apt to be cross;" said I; "we must bear with it as we do with the eccentricities of genius; besides, when she gets accustomed to us, it will be better."

Madam was therefore installed into her pretty pasture-lot, and my wife contemplated with pleasure the picturesque effect of her appearance reclining on the green slope of the pasture-lot, or standing ancle-deep in the gurgling brook, or reclining under the deep shadows of the trees—she was, in fact, a handsome cow, which may account, in part, for some of her sins; and this consideration inspired me with some degree of indulgence toward her foibles.

But when I found that Biddy could never succeed in getting near her in the pasture, and that any kind of success in the milking operations required my vigorous personal exertions morning and evening, the matter wore a more serious as-

pect, and I began to feel quite pensive and appre-
hensive. It is very well to talk of the pleasures
of the milkmaid going out in the balmy freshness
of the purple dawn; but imagine a poor fellow
pulled out of bed on a drizzly, rainy morning, and
equipping himself for a scamper through a wet
pasture-lot, rope in hand, at the heels of such a
termagant as mine! In fact, madam established
a regular series of exercises, which had all to be
gone through before she would suffer herself to
be captured; as, first, she would station herself
plump in the middle of a marsh, which lay at the
lower part of the lot, and look very innocent and
absent-minded, as if reflecting on some sentimen-
tal subject. "Suke! Suke! Suke!" I ejaculate
cautiously, tottering along the edge of the marsh,
and holding out an ear of corn. The lady looks
gracious, and comes forward, almost within reach
of my hand. I make a plunge to throw the rope
over her horns, and away she goes, kicking up
mud and water into my face in her flight, while I,
losing my balance, tumble forward into the marsh.
I pick myself up, and, full of wrath, behold her
placidly chewing the cud on the other side, with
the meekest air imaginable, as who should say,

"I hope you are not hurt, sir." I dash through swamp and bog furiously, resolving to carry all by *coup de main*. Then follows a miscellaneous season of dodging, scampering, and bo-peeping among the trees of the grove, interspersed with sundry occasional races across the bog aforesaid. I always wondered how I caught her every day, when I had tied her head to one post and her heels to another, I wiped the sweat from my brow and thought I was paying dear for the eccentricities of genius. A genius she certainly was, for besides her surprising agility, she had other talents equally extraordinary. There was no fence that she could not take down; nowhere that she could not go. She took the pickets off the garden fence at her pleasure, using her horns as handily as I could use a claw hammer. Whatever she has a mind to, whether it were a bite in the cabbage garden, or a run in the corn patch, or a foraging expedition into the flower borders, she made herself equally welcome and at home. Such a scampering and driving, such cries of "Suke here" and "Suke there," as constantly greeted our ears kept our little establishment in a constant commotion. At last, when she one morning made a plunge at the skirts of a new broadcloth frock coat, and carried off one flap on her horns, my patience gave out, and I determined to sell her.

As, however, I had made a good story of my misfortunes among my friends and neighbours, and amused them with sundry whimsical accounts of my various adventures in the cow-catching line, I found when I came to speak of selling, that there was a general coolness on the subject, and nobody seemed disposed to be the recipient of my responsibilities. In short, I was glad, at last, to get fifteen dollars for her, and comforted myself with thinking that I had at least gained twenty-five dollars' worth of experience in the transaction, to say nothing of the fine exercise.

I comforted my soul, however, the day after, by purchasing and bringing home to my wife a fine swarm of bees.

"Your bee, now," says I, "is a really classical insect, and breathes of Virgil and the Augustan age—and then, she is a domestic, tranquil, placid creature! How beautiful the murmuring of a hive near our honeysuckle of a calm summer evening! Then they are tranquilly and peacefully amassing for us their stores of sweetness, while they lull us with their murmurs. What a beautiful image of disinterested benevolence!"

My wife declared that I was quite a poet, and the bee-hive was duly installed near the flower-pots, that the delicate creatures might have the full benefit of the honeysuckle and mignonette. My spirits began to rise. I bought three different treatises on the rearing of bees, and also one or two new patterns of hives, and proposed to rear my bees on the most approved model. I charged all the establishment to let me know when there was any indication of an emigrating spirit, that I might be ready to receive the new swarm into my patent mansion.

Accordingly, one afternoon, when I was deep in an article that I was preparing for the *North American Review*, intelligence was brought me that a swarm had risen. I was on the alert at once, and discovered on going out that the provoking creatures had chosen the top of a tree about thirty feet high to settle on. Now, my books had carefully instructed me just how to approach the swarm and cover them with a new hive, but I had never contemplated the possibility of the swarm being, like Haman's gallows, forty cubits high.

I looked despairingly upon the smooth-bark tree, which rose like a column, full twenty feet, without branch or twig. "What is to be done?" said I, appealing to two or three neighbours. At last, at the recommendation of one of them, a ladder was raised against the tree, and, equipped with a shirt outside of my clothes, a green veil over my head, and a pair of leather gloves in my hand, I went up with a saw at my girdle to saw off the branch on which they had settled, and lower it by a rope to a neighbour, similarly equipped, who stood below with the hive.

As a result of this manœuvre the fastidious little insects were at length fairly installed at housekeeping in my new patent hive, and, rejoicing in my success, I again sat down to my article.

That evening my wife and I took tea in our honeysuckle arbour, with our little ones and a friend or two, to whom I showed my treasures, and expatiated at large on the comforts and conveniences of the new patent hive.

But alas for the hopes of man! The little ungrateful wretches, what must they do but take advantage of my oversleeping myself the next morning, to clear out for new quarters without so much

as leaving me a P. P. C. Such was the fact; at
eight o'clock I found the new patent hive as good
as ever; but the bees I have never seen from that
day to this!

"The rascally little conservatives!" said I; "I
believe that they have never had a new idea from
the days of Virgil down, and are entirely unpre-
pared to appreciate improvements."

Meanwhile the seeds began to germinate in our
garden, when we found, to our chagrin, that, between John Bull and Paddy, there had occurred
sundry confusions in the several departments.
Radishes had been planted broadcast, carrots and
beets arranged in hills, and here and there a
whole paper of seed appeared to have been planted
bodily. My good old uncle, who, somewhat to my
confusion, made me a call at this time, was greatly
distressed and scandalized by the appearance of
our garden. But, by a deal of fussing, transplant-
ing, and replanting, it was got into some shape and
order. My uncle was rather troublesome, as careful old people are apt to be—annoying us by per-
petual inquiries of what we gave for this, and that,
and running up provoking calculations on the
final cost of matters, and we began to wish that

his visit might be as short as would be convenient.

But when, on taking leave, he promised to send us a fine young cow of his own raising, our hearts rather smote us for our impatience.

"'Taint any of your new breeds, nephew," said the old man, "yet I can say that she's a gentle, likely young crittur, and better worth forty dollars than many a one that's cried up for Ayrshire or Durham; and you shall be quite welcome to her."

We thanked him, as in duty bound, and thought that if he was full of old-fashioned notions, he was no less full of kindness and good will.

And now, with a new cow, with our garden beginning to thrive under the gentle showers of May, with our flower-borders blooming, my wife and I began to think ourselves in Paradise. But alas! the same sun and rain that warmed our fruit and flowers brought up from the earth, like sulky gnomes, a vast array of purple-leaved weeds, that almost in a night seemed to cover the whole surface of the garden beds. Our gardeners both being gone, the weeding was expected to be done by me—one of the anticipated relaxations of my leisure hours.

4

"Well," said I, in reply to a gentle intimation from my wife, "when my article is finished, I'll take a day and weed all up clean."

Thus days slipped by, till at length the article was dispatched, and I proceeded to my garden. Amazement! who could have possibly foreseen that anything earthly could grow so fast in a few days! There were no bounds, no alleys, no beds, no distinction of beet and carrot, nothing but a flourishing congregation of weeds nodding and bobbing in the morning breeze, as if to say,—"We hope you are well, sir—we've got the ground, you see!" I began to explore, and to hoe, and to weed. Ah! did anybody ever try to clean a neglected carrot or beet bed, or bend his back in a hot sun over rows of weedy onions! He is the man to feel for my despair! How I weeded, and sweat, and sighed! till, when high noon came on, as the result of all my toils, only three beds were cleaned! And how disconsolate looked the good seed, thus unexpectedly delivered from its sheltering tares, and laid open to a broiling July sun! Every juvenile beet and carrot lay flat down, wilted and drooping, as if, like me, they had been weeding instead of being weeded.

"This weeding is quite a serious matter," said I to my wife; "the fact is, I must have help about it!"

"Just what I was myself thinking," said my wife. "My flower-borders are all in confusion, and my petunia mounds so completely overgrown, that nobody would dream what they were meant for!"

In short it was agreed between us that we could not afford the expense of a full-grown man to keep our place, yet we must reinforce ourselves by the addition of a boy, and a brisk youngster from the vicinity was pitched upon as the happy addition. This youth was a fellow of decidedly quick parts, and in one forenoon made such a clearing in our garden that I was delighted—bed after bed appeared to view, all cleared and dressed out with such celerity that I was quite ashamed of my own slowness, until, on examination, I discovered that he had, with great impartiality, pulled up both weeds and vegetables.

This hopeful beginning was followed up by a succession of proceedings which should be recorded for the instruction of all who seek for help from the race of boys. Such a loser of all tools, great

and small—such an invariable leaver-open of all
gates, and a letter down of bars—such a personi-
fication of all manner of anarchy and ill luck—
had never before been seen on the estate. His
time, while I was gone to the city, was agreeably
diversified with roosting on the fence, swinging on
the gates, making poplar whistles for the children,
hunting eggs, and eating whatever fruit happened
to be in season, in which latter accomplishment he
was certainly quite distinguished. After about
three weeks of this kind of joint gardening, we
concluded to dismiss master Tom from the firm,
and employ a man.

"Things must be taken care of," said I, "and
I cannot do it. 'Tis out of the question." And
so the man was secured.

But I am making a long story, and may chance
to outrun the sympathies of my readers. Time
would fail me to tell of the distresses manifold
that fell upon me—of cows dried up by poor
milkers, of hens that wouldn't set at all, and hens
that despite all law and reason wonld set on one
egg, of hens that having hatched families straight-
way led them into all manner of high grass and
weeds, by which means numerous young chicks

caught premature colds and perished! and how when I, with manifold toil, had driven one of these inconsiderate gadders into a coop, to teach her domestic habits, the rats came down upon her, and slew every chick in one night! how my pigs were always practising gymnastic exercises over the fence of the stye, and marauding in the garden. (I wonder that Fourier never conceived the idea of having his garden-land ploughed by pigs, for certainly they manifest quite a decided elective attraction for turning up the earth.)

When autumn came, I went soberly to market in the neighbouring city, and bought my potatoes and turnips like any other man, for, between all the various systems of gardening pursued, I was obliged to confess that my first horticultural effort was a decided failure. But though all my rural visions had proved illusive, there were some very substantial realities. My bill at the seed store, for seeds, roots, and tools, for example, had run up to an amount that was perfectly unaccountable; then there were various smaller items, such as horse-shoeing, carriage-mending—for he who lives in the country and does business in the city must keep his vehicle and appurtenances. I had always prided myself on being an exact man, and settling every account, great and small, with the going out of the old year, but this season I found myself sorely put to it. In fact, had not I received a timely lift from my good old uncle, I had made a complete break-down. The old gentleman's troublesome habit of ciphering and calculating, it seems, had led him beforehand to foresee that I was not exactly in the money-making line, nor likely to possess much surplus revenue to meet the note which I had given for my place, and therefore he quietly paid it himself, as I discovered when, after much anxiety and some sleepless nights, I went to the holder to ask for an extension of credit.

"He was right after all," said I to my wife, "'to live cheap in the country, a body must know how.'"

Children.

"A little child shall lead them."

One cold market morning I looked into a milliner's shop, and there I saw a hale, hearty, well-browned young fellow from the country, with his long cart whip, and lion shag coat, holding up some little matter, and turning it about on his great fist. And what do you suppose it was? *A baby's bonnet!* A little, soft, blue satin hood, with a swan's down border, white as the new fallen snow, with a frill of rich blonde around the edge.

By his side stood a very pretty woman holding, with no small pride, the baby—for evidently it was the baby. Any one could read that fact in every glance, as they looked at each other, and then at the large unconscious eyes, and fat dimpled cheeks of the little one.

It was evident that neither of them had ever seen a baby like that before.

"But really, Mary," said the young man, "isn't three dollars very high?"

Mary very prudently said nothing, but taking

the little bonnet, tied it on the little head, and held up the little baby. The man looked, and without another word down went the three dollars; all that the last week's butter came to; and as they walked out of the shop, it is hard to say which looked the most delighted with the bargain.

"Ah," thought I, "a little child shall lead them."

Another day, as I was passing a carriage factory along one of our principal back streets, I saw a young mechanic at work on a wheel. The rough body of a carriage stood beside him, and there, wrapped up snugly, all hooded and cloaked, sat a little dark-eyed girl, about a year old, playing with a great shaggy dog. As I stopped, the man looked up from his work and turned admiringly toward his little companion, as much as to say, "See what I have got here!"

"Yes," thought I, "and if the little lady ever gets a glance from admiring swains as sincere as that, she will be lucky."

Ah! these children, little witches, pretty even in all their faults and absurdities. See, for example, yonder little fellow in a haughty fit; he has shaken his long curls over his deep blue eyes; the fair brow is bent in a frown; the rose-leaf lip is pursed up in infinite defiance; and the white shoulder thrust naughtily forward. Can any but a child look so pretty, even in their naughtiness?

Then comes the instant change; flashing smiles and tears, as the good comes back all in a rush, and you are overwhelmed with protestations, promises, and kisses! They are irresistible, too, these little ones. They pull away the scholar's pen; tumble about his paper; make somersets over his books; and what can he do? They tear up newspapers; litter the carpets; break, pull, and upset, and then jabber unimaginable English in self-defiance, and what can you do for yourself?

"If I had a child," says the precise man, "you should see."

He does have a child, and his child tears up his papers, tumbles over his things, and pulls his nose, like all other children, and what has the precise man to say for himself? Nothing; he is like every body else; "a little child may lead him."

The hardened heart of the worldly man is unlocked by the guileless tones and simple caresses of his son; but he repays it in time, by imparting to his boy all the crooked tricks and callous maxims which have undone himself.

Go to the jail—to the penitentiary, and find there the wretch most sullen, brutal, and hardened. Then look at your infant son. Such as he is to you, such to some mother was this man. That hard hand was soft and delicate; that rough voice was tender and lisping; fond eyes followed him as he played, and he was rocked and cradled as something holy. There was a time when his heart, soft and unworn, might have opened to questionings of God and Jesus, and been sealed with the seal of Heaven. But harsh hands seized it; fierce goblin lineaments were impressed upon it; and all is over with him forever!

So of the tender, weeping child, is made the callous, heartless man; of the all-believing child, the sneering sceptic; of the beautiful and modest, the shameless and abandoned; and this is what *the world* does for the little one.

There was a time when the *divine One* stood on earth, and little children sought to draw near to him. But harsh human beings stood between him and them, forbidding their approach. Ah! has it not always been so? Do not even we with our hard and unsubdued feeling, our worldly and unscriptural habits and maxims, stand like a dark screen between our little child and its Saviour, and keep even from the choice bud of our hearts, the sweet radiance which might unfold it for paradise? "Suffer little children to come unto me, and forbid them not," is still the voice of the Son of God, but the cold world still closes around and forbids. When of old, disciples would question their Lord of the higher mysteries of his kingdom, he took a little child and set him in the midst, as a sign of him who should be greatest in Heaven. That gentle teacher remains still to us. By every hearth and fireside, Jesus still *sets the little child in the midst of us.*

Wouldst thou know, O parent, what is that *faith* which unlocks heaven? Go not to wrangling polemics, or creeds and forms of theology, but draw to thy bosom thy little one, and read in that clear trusting eye the lesson of eternal life. Be only to thy God as thy child is to thee, and all is done! Blessed shalt thou be indeed, " *when a little child shall lead thee !*"

The Two Bibles.

It was a splendid room. Rich curtains swept down to the floor in graceful folds, half excluding the light, and shedding it in soft hues over the fine old paintings on the walls, and over the broad mirrors that reflect all that taste can accomplish by the hand of wealth. Books, the rarest and most costly, were around, in every form of gorgeous binding and gilding, and among them, glittering in ornament, lay a magnificent Bible—a Bible too beautiful in its appearance, too showy, too ornamental, ever to have been meant to be read—a Bible which every visitor should take up, and exclaim, "What a beautiful edition! what superb binding!" and then lay it down again.

And the master of the house was lounging on a sofa, looking over a late review—for he was a man of leisure, taste, and reading—but then, as to reading the Bible!—that forms, we suppose, no part of the pretensions of a man of letters. The Bible—certainly he considered it a very respecta-

84

ble book—a fine specimen of ancient literature, an admirable book of moral precepts—but then, as to its divine origin he had not exactly made up his mind—some parts appeared strange and inconsistent to his reason, others were very revolting to his taste—true, he had never studied it very attentively, yet such was his general impression about it—but on the whole, he thought it well enough to keep an elegant copy of it on his drawing-room table.

So much for one picture, now for another.

Come with us into this little dark alley, and up a flight of ruinous stairs. It is a bitter night, and the wind and snow might drive through the crevices of the poor room, were it not that careful hands have stopped them with paper or cloth. But for all this little carefulness, the room is bitter cold—cold even with those few decaying brands on the hearth, which that sorrowful woman is trying to kindle with her breath. Do you see that pale little thin girl, with large bright eyes, who is crouching so near her mother? hark! how she coughs—now listen:

"Mary, my dear child," says the mother, "do keep that shawl close about you, you are cold, I know," and the woman shivers as she speaks.

"No, mother, not very," replies the child, again relapsing into that hollow, ominous cough—"I wish you wouldn't make me always wear your shawl when it is cold, mother."

"Dear child, you need it most—how you cough to-night," replies the mother, "it really don't seem right for me to send you up that long street, now your shoes have grown so poor; I must go myself after this."

"Oh! mother, you must stay with the baby; what if he should have one of those dreadful fits while you are gone; no, I can go very well, I have got used to the cold, now."

"But, mother, I'm cold," says a little voice from the scanty bed in the corner, "mayn't I get up and come to the fire?"

"Dear child, it would not warm you—it is very cold here, and I can't make any more fire to-night."

"Why can't you, mother? there are four whole sticks of wood in the box, do put one on, and let's get warm once."

"No, my dear little Henry," says the mother,

soothingly, "that is all the wood mother has, and I haven't any money to get more."

And now wakens the sick baby in the little cradle, and mother and daughter are both for some time busy in attempting to supply its little wants, and lulling it again to sleep.

And now look you well at that mother. Six months ago she had a husband, whose earnings procured for her both the necessaries and comforts of life—her children were clothed, fed, and schooled, without thought of hers. But husbandless and alone, in the heart of a great busy city, with feeble health, and only the precarious resources of her needle, she had come rapidly down from comfort to extreme poverty. Look at her now, as she is to-night. She knows full well that the pale bright-eyed girl, whose hollow cough constantly rings in her ears, is far from well. She knows that cold, and hunger, and exposure of every kind, are daily and surely wearing away her life, and yet what can she do? Poor soul, how many times has she calculated all her little resources, to see if she could pay a doctor, and get medicine for Mary—yet all in vain. She knows that timely medicine, ease, fresh air, and warmth,

might save her—but she knows that all these
things are out of the question for her.   She feels,
too, as a mother would feel, when she sees her
once rosy, happy little boy, becoming pale, and
anxious, and fretful; and even when he teases her
most, she only stops her work a moment, and
strokes his poor little thin cheeks, and thinks what
a laughing, happy little fellow he once was, till
she has not a heart to reprove him.   And all this
day she has toiled with a sick and fretful baby in
her lap, and her little, shivering, hungry boy at
her side, whom poor Mary's patient artifices cannot always keep quiet; she has toiled over the last
piece of work which she can procure from the
shop, for the man has told her that after this he
can furnish no more.   And the little money that
is to come from this is already proportioned out
in her mind, and after that she has no human
prospect of more.

But yet the woman's face is patient, quiet, firm.
Nay, you may even see in her suffering eye something like peace; and whence comes it?   I will
tell you.

There is a Bible in that room, as well as in the
rich man's apartment.   Not splendidly bound, to

be sure, but faithfully read—a plain, homely, much worn book.

Hearken now, while she says to her children, "Listen to me, my dear children, and I will read you something out of this book. 'Let not your heart be troubled, in my Father's house are many mansions.' So you see, my children, we shall not always live in this little, cold, dark room. Jesus Christ has promised to take us to a better home."

"Shall we be warm there, all day?" says the little boy earnestly, "and shall we have enough to eat?"

"Yes, dear child," says the mother, "listen to what the Bible says, 'They shall hunger no more, neither thirst any more, for the Lamb which is in the midst of them shall feed them; and God shall wipe away all tears from their eyes.'"

"I am glad of that," said little Mary, "for mother, I never can bear to see you cry."

"But, mother," says little Henry, "won't God send us something to eat to-morrow?"

"See," says the mother, "what the Bible says, 'Seek ye not what ye shall eat, nor what ye shall drink, neither be of anxious mind. For your Father knoweth that ye have need of these things.

"But, mother," says little Mary, "if God is

our Father, and loves us, what does he let us be so poor for?"

"Nay," says the mother, "our Lord Jesus Christ was as poor as we are, and God certainly loved him."

"Was he, mother?"

"Yes, children, you remember how he said, 'The Son of Man hath not where to lay his head.' And it tells us more than once, that Jesus was hungry when there was none to give him food."

"Oh! mother, what should we do without the Bible!" says Mary.

Now if the rich man who had not yet made up his mind what to think of the Bible, should visit this poor woman, and ask her on what she grounded her belief of its truth, what could she answer? Could she give the argument from miracles and prophecy? Can she account for all the changes which might have taken place in it through translators and copyists, and prove that we have a genuine and uncorrupted version? Not she! But how then does she know that it is true? How, say you? How does she know that she has warm life-blood in her heart? How does she know that there is such a thing as air and sunshine?

She does not *believe* these things, she *knows* them; and in like manner, with a deep heart-consciousness, she is certain that the words of her Bible are truth and life. Is it by reasoning that the frightened child, bewildered in the dark, knows its mother's voice? No! Nor is it by reasoning that the forlorn and distressed human heart knows the voice of its Saviour, and is still.

Go when the child is lying in its mother's arms, and looking up trustfully in her face, and see if you can puzzle him with metaphysical difficulties about personal identity, until you can make him think that it is not his mother. Your reasonings may be conclusive—your arguments unanswerable—but after all, the child sees his mother there, and feels her arms around him, and his quiet unreasoning belief on the subject, is precisely of the same kind which the little child of Christianity feels in the existence of his Saviour, and the reality of all those blessed truths which he has told in his word.

Letter from Maine.—No. 1.

THE fashionable complaint of neuralgia has kept back from your paper many "thoughts, motions, and revolutions" of the brain, which, could they have printed themselves on paper, would have found their way towards you. Don't you suppose, in the marvellous progress of this fast-living age, the time will ever come, when, by some metaphysical daguerreotype process, the thoughts and images of the brain shall print themselves on paper, without the intervention of pen and ink? Then, how many brilliancies, now lost and forgotten before one gets time to put them through the slow process of writing, shall flash upon us! Our poets will sit in luxurious ease, with a quire of paper in their pockets, and have nothing to do but lean back in their chairs, and go off in an ecstacy, and lo! they will find it all written out, commas and all, ready for the printer. What a relief, too, to

multitudes of gentle hearts, whose friends in this
busy age are too hurried to find much time for
writing. Your merchant puts a sheet of paper in-
side of his vest—over his heart, of course—and in
the interval between selling goods and pricing
stocks, thinks warm thoughts towards his wife or
lady-love—and at night draws forth a long letter,
all directed for the post. How convenient!
Would that some friend of humanity would offer a
premium for the discovery!

The spiritual rapping fraternity, who are *au fait*
in all that relates to man's capabilities, and who
are now speaking *ex cathedra* of all things celes-
tial and terrestrial, past, present, and to come, can
perhaps immediately settle the minutiæ of such an
arrangement. One thing is quite certain : that
if every man wore a sheet of paper in his bosom,
on which there should be a true and literal version of all his thoughts, even for one day, in a
great many cases he would be astounded on reading it over. Are there not many who would there
see, in plain, unvarnished English, what their
patriotism, disinterestedness, generosity, friend-
ship, and religion actually amounts to? Let us
fancy some of our extra patriotic public men com-

paring such a sheet with their speeches. We have been amused, sometimes, at the look of blank astonishment with which men look for the first time on their own daguerreotype. Is that me? Do I look so? Perhaps this *inner* daguerreotype might prove more surprising still. "What, *I* think *that?* I purpose so—and so? What a troublesome ugly machine! I'll have nothing to do with it!"

But to drop that subject, and start another. It seems to us quite wonderful, that in all the ecstacies that have been lavished on American scenery, this beautiful State of Maine should have been so much neglected; for nothing is or can be more wildly, peculiarly beautiful—particularly the scenery of the sea-coast. A glance at the map will show one the peculiarity of these shores. It is a complicated network and labyrinth of islands— the sea interpenetrating the land in every fanciful form, through a belt of coast from fifteen to twenty miles wide. The effect of this, as it lies on the map, and as it lives and glows in reality, is as different as the difference between the poetry of life and its dead matter of fact.

But supposing yourself almost anywhere in

Maine, within fifteen miles of the shore, and you
start for a ride to the sea side, you will then be in
a fair way to realize it.   The sea, living, beautiful, and life-giving, seems, as you ride, to be
everywhere about you—behind, before, around.
Now it rises like a lake, gemmed with islands, and
embosomed by rich swells of woodland.   Now
you catch a peep of it on your right hand, among
tufts of oak and maple, and anon it spreads on
your left to a majestic sheet of silver, among rocky
shores, hung with dark pines, hemlocks, and
spruces.

The sea shores of Connecticut and Massachusetts have a kind of baldness and barenness which
you never see here.   As you approach the ocean
there, the trees seem to become stunted and few
in number, but *here* the sea luxuriates, swells, and
falls, in the very lap of the primeval forest.
The tide water washes the drooping branches of
the oak and maple, and dashes itself up into whole
hedges of luxuriant arbor vitæ.

No language can be too enthusiastic to paint the
beauty of the evergreens in these forests   The
lordly spruce, so straight, so tall, so perfectly de-
fined in its outline, with its regal crest of cones

sparkling with the clear exuded gum, and bearing
on its top that "silent finger" which Elliot de-
scribes as " ever pointing up to God"—the ancient
white pine with its slender whispering leaves, the
feathery larches, the rugged and shaggy cedars—
all unite to form such a " goodly fellowship," that
one is inclined to think for the time that no son
of the forest can compare with them.   But the
spruce is the prince among them all. Far or
near, you see its slender obelisk of dark green,
rising singly amid forests of oak or maple, or mar-
shalled together in serried ranks over distant hills,
or wooding innumerable points, whose fantastic
outlines interlace the silvery sea.   The heavy
blue green of these distant pines forms a beautiful
contrast to the glitter of the waters, and affords a
fine background, to throw out the small white
wings of sail boats, which are ever passing from
point to point among these bays and harbors.
One of the most peculiar and romantic features
of these secluded wood-embosomed waters of
Maine is this sudden apparition of shipping and
sea craft, in such wild and lonely places, that they
seem to you, as the first ships did to the simple
savages, to be visitants from the spirit land.

You are riding in a lonely road, by some bay that seems to you like a secluded inland lake; you check your horse, to notice the fine outline of the various points, when lo! from behind one of them, swan-like, with wings all spread, glides in a ship from India or China, and wakes up the silence, by tumbling her great anchor into the water. A ship, of itself a child of romance—a dreamy, cloud-like, poetic thing—and that ship connects these piney hills and rocky shores, these spruces and firs, with distant lands of palm and spice, and speaks to you, in these solitudes, of groves of citron and olive. We pray the day may never come when any busy Yankee shall find a substitute for ship sails, and take from these spirits of the wave their glorious white wings, and silent, cloud-like movements, for any fuss and sputter of steam and machinery. It will be just like some Yankee to do it. That race will never rest till everything antique and poetic is drilled out of the world. The same spirit which yearns to make Niagara a mill-seat, and use all its pomp and power of cloud, and spray, and rainbow, and its voices of many waters, for accessories to a cotton factory, would, we suppose, be right glad to trans-

form the winged ship into some disagreeable
greasy combination of machinery, if it would only
come cheaper. The islands along the coast of
Maine are a study for a tourist. The whole sail
along the shores is through a never ending
labyrinth of these—some high and rocky, with
castellated sides, bannered with pines—some rich-
ly wooded with forest trees—and others, again,
whose luxuriant meadow land affords the finest
pasturage for cattle. Here are the cottages of
fishermen, who divide their time between farming
and fishing, and thus between land and water
make a very respectable amphibious living. These
people are simple-hearted, kindly, hardy, with a
good deal of the genial broad-heartedness that
characterizes their old father, the ocean. When
down on one of these lonely islands once, we
were charmed to find, in a small cottage, one of
the prettiest and most lady-like of women. Her
husband owned a fishing-smack; and while we
were sitting conversing in the house, in came a
damsel from the neighborhood, arrayed, in all
points, *cap-a-pie*, according to the latest city
fashions. The husband came home from a trip
while we were there. He had stopped in Portland,

and brought home a new bonnet for his wife, of the most approved style, and a pair of gaiter shoes for his little girl. One of our company was talking with him, congratulating him on his retired situation.

"You can go all about, trading in your vessel, and making money," he said, "and here on this retired island there is no way to spend it, so you must lay up a good deal."

"Don't know about that," said the young man; "there's women and girls everywhere; and they must have their rings, and their pins, and parasols and ribbons. There's ways enough for money to go."

On Sunday mornings, these islanders have out their sail-boats, and all make sail for some point where there is a church. They spend the day in religious service, and return at evening. Could one wish a more picturesque way of going to meeting of a calm summer morning?

So beautiful a country, one would think, must have nurtured the poetic sentiment; and Maine, accordingly, has given us one of our truest poets—Longfellow. Popular as his poetry is, on a first reading, it is poetry that improves and grows on

one by acquaintance and study; and more particularly should be studied under the skies and
by the seas of that State whose beauty first inspired it.   No one who views the scenery of
Maine artistically, and then studies the poems
of Longfellow, can avoid seeing that its hues and
tones, its beautiful word-painting, and the exquisite
variety and smoothness of its cadences, have been
caught, not from books and study, but from a
long and deep *heart* communion with Nature.
We recollect seeing with some indignation, a few
years ago, what seemed to us a very captious criticism on Longfellow; and it simply occurred to
us then, that if the critic had spent as much time
in the forest as the poet, and become as familiar
with the fine undertones of Nature, such a critique
never would have appeared.   A lady who has
lately been rambling with us among the scenery
of Maine, and reading Longfellow's poems, said,
the other day—"He must have learned his measure from the sea; there is just its beautiful ripple
in all his verses"—a very beautiful and very just
criticism.   There are some fine lines in Evange-
line, that give us the pine forests of Maine like a
painting :

" This is the forest primeval—the murmuring pines and
the hemlocks

Bearded with moss and with garments green, indistinct
in the twilight

Stand like Druids of Eld, with voices sad and prophetic,

Stand like harpers hoar, with beards that rest on their
bosoms:

Loud from its rocky caverns, the deep-voiced neighboring
ocean

Speaks, and in accents disconsolate answers the wail of the
forest."

Drawn to the very life! We have seen those
very Druids—graybeards, dusky garments and
all, on the shores of Maine, many a time; and if
anybody wants to feel the beauty and grandeur
of the picture, he must go to some of those wild
rocky islands there.

Longfellow's poetry has the true seal of the
bard in this: that while it is dyed rich as an old
cathedral window in tints borrowed in foreign
language and literature—tints caught in the fields
of Spain, Italy, and Germany—yet, after all, the
strong dominant colors are from fields and scenes
of home. So truly is he a poet of Maine, that we
could wish to see his poems in every fisherman's
cottage, through all the wild islands, and among

all the romantic bays and creeks of that beautiful shore.

It would be a fine critical study to show how this undertone of native imagery and feeling passes through all that singular harmony which the poet's scholarcraft has enabled him to compose from the style of many nations; and some day we have it in heart to do this in a future letter. At present we will not bestow any further tediousness upon you.

Very truly,   H. B. S.

Letter from Maine.—No. 2.

THE *last* letter from Maine! how painful a word this may be, only those who can fully appreciate this beautiful, hospitable, noble-hearted State, can say.

Maine stands as a living disproval of the received opinion, that Northern latitudes chill the blood, or check the flow of warm and social feeling. There is a fullness, a frankness, and freedom, combined with simplicity, about the social and domestic life of this State, which reminds me of the hospitality and generosity of Kentucky, more than anything else, and yet has added to it that stability and intelligent firmness peculiar to the atmosphere of New England. Perhaps it is because Maine, like Kentucky, is yet but a half-settled State, and has still a kind of pioneer, backwoods atmosphere about it. All impulses which come from the great heart of nature, from the woods, the mountains, or the ocean, are al-

(103)

ways pure and generous—and those influences in Maine are yet stronger than the factitious second-hand and man-made influences of artificial life.

Truly, whether we consider the natural beauty of Maine, or the intellectual clearness and development of her common people, or the unsophisticated simplicity of life and manners there, or the late glorious example which she has set in the eyes of all the nations of the earth, one must say she is well worthy of her somewhat aspiring motto—the North Star! and the significant word, "Dirigo!"

DIRIGO. That word is getting to have, in this day, a fullness of meaning, that perhaps was not contemplated when it was assumed into her escutcheon—for Maine is indeed the North Star, and the guiding hand in a movement that is to *regenerate all nations*—and from all nations the cry for her guidance begins to be heard.

It is said that the very mention of the State of Maine, in temperance gatherings in England, now raises tumults of applause, and that *Neal Dow* has been sent for even as far as Berlin, to carry the light of this new gospel of peace on earth, and good will to men.

The last election in Maine, taken altogether, is the most magnificent triumph of principle, *pure* principle, that the world ever saw. Thousands and tens of thousands of money had been sent by liquor dealers in other States to bribe voters—it had been triumphantly asserted that votes in Maine could be had for *two dollars a head*—but when they came to try the thing practically upon her sturdy old farmers and fishermen, they then got quite a new idea of what a Maine man was. The old aquatic farmers, who inherit all the noble traits both of sea and land, shook their hands most emphatically from holding bribes, and the mountain farmers showed that in the course of their agricultural life and experiments they had learned, among other things, the striking difference between *wheat and chaff*. No! no! bribing was plainly "no go" in Maine; the money was only taken by a few poor, harmless loafers, of the kind who roost on rail fences on a sunny day, or lean up against barns, when for obvious reasons they are in no condition to roost, and who are especially interested in the question of the rights of women to saw wood.

The *election in Maine* is an *era* in the history

5 *

of elections, because there, for once, men of principle forsook all party lines and measures, to vote for PRINCIPLE alone. Whigs voted for Democrats, Democrats for Whigs, with sole reference to their relation to the temperance cause, and thus a great and memorable victory was gained. *Party* is the great Anti-Christ of a republican government, and the discipline of party has hitherto been so stringent that it really has been impossible to determine the sentiment of a Christian man by his vote, except so far as it might signify the opinion of the party with which they were connected. Maine, in agreement with her motto, "*Dirigo,*" has set the example of two very great and important things. One is, that this traffic may be suppressed by law; and the other is, that men of principle can vote out of their party—and the second suggestion is quite equal in value with the first. For if men can vote out of their party for one great question of right, they can for another; and the time is not distant, we trust, when the noble State of Maine will apply the same liberty to other subjects.

While I have been writing this, an invisible spirit has been walking in our forests, and lo, the change! The serrated ranks of spruces are lighted with brilliant forms of trees, flame coloured, yellow, scarlet, all shining out between the un-changed steel blue of the old evergreens. If one wants the perfection of American forest scenery, he must have for the rainbow illumination of au-tumn, a background of sombre black green like ours. Fancy the graceful indentations, the thou-sand lake-like beautiful bays of this charming shore, now reflecting in their mirror this hourly brightening. pageant—fancy the ships gliding in and out from Jeddo, China, California, England! and you can fancy the regret and longing of heart with which I leave a coast so beautiful. Fancy that you see dwellings, speaking alike of simplicity and of refinement—imagine families where intelligence, heartiness, warm hospitality, and true Christian principle, all conspire to make your visit a pleasure, and your departure a regret, and you can fancy a more intimate reason of the sorrow with which I write myself no longer a resi-dent of that State. But as I leave it, I cannot but express the wish that every family, and every individual may remember the glory which their State has now, and the character which it has now to sustain in the eyes of the whole civilized world.

The women of Maine have had no small influence in deciding the triumph of the cause which sheds such lustre on their State. All women, as a natural thing, are friends and advocates of the cause of temperance, a cause involving so much to sons, brothers, and husbands; and the Maine women have acted most decidedly and nobly in its support.

To the "*North Star*," now the eyes of all the world are turning, and we must look to it to guide us in everything that is right and noble. May that star be seen as plainly leading the generous cause of freedom! that cause whose full success shall wipe from the American escutcheon its only national stain.   H. E. B. S.

Christmas, or the Good Fairy.

"OH, dear! Christmas is coming in a fortnight, and I have got to think up presents for everybody!" said young Ellen Stuart, as she leaned languidly back in her chair. "Dear me! it's so tedious! Everybody has got everything that can be thought of."

"Oh, no!" said her confidential adviser, Miss Lester, in a soothing tone. "You have means of buying everything you can fancy, and when every shop and store is glittering with all manner of splendors, you cannot surely be at a loss."

"Well, now, just listen. To begin with, there's mamma! what can I get for her? I have thought of ever so many things. She has three card-cases, four gold thimbles, two or three gold chains, two writing desks of different patterns; and then, as to rings, brooches, boxes, and all other things, I should think she might be sick of the sight of them. I am sure I am," said she, languidly gazing on her white and jewelled fingers.

This view of the case seemed rather puzzling to the adviser, and there was silence for a few moments, when Eleanor, yawning, resumed—

"And then there's cousins Ellen and Mary—I suppose they will be coming down on me with a whole load of presents; and Mrs. B. will send me something—she did last year; and then there's cousins William and Tom—I must get them something, and I would like to do it well enough, if I only knew what to get!

"Well," said Eleanor's aunt, who had been sitting quietly rattling her knitting needles during this speech, "it's a pity that you had not such a subject to practice on as I was when I was a girl —presents did not fly about in those days as they do now. I remember when I was ten years old, my father gave sister Mary and me a most marvellously ugly sugar dog for a Christmas gift, and we were perfectly delighted with it—the very idea of a present was so new to us."

"Dear aunt, how delighted I should be if I had any such fresh unsophisticated body to get presents for! but to get and get for people that have more than they know what to do with now—to add pictures, books, and gilding, when the centre-tables are loaded with them now—and rings and jewels, when they are a perfect drug! I wish myself that I were not sick, and sated, and tired with having everything in the world given me!"

"Well, Eleanor," said her aunt, "if you really do want unsophisticated subjects to practise on, I can put you in the way of it. I can show you more than one family to whom you might seem to be a very good fairy, and where such gifts as you could give with all ease would seem like a magic dream."

"Why, that would really be worth while, aunt."

"Look right across the way," said her aunt. "You see that building."

"That miserable combination of shanties? Yes!"

"Well, I have several acquaintances there who have never been tired of Christmas gifts, or gifts of any other kind. I assure you, you could make quite a sensation over there."

"Well, who is there? Let us know!'

"Do you remember Owen, that used to make your shoes?"

"Yes, I remember something about him."

"Well, he has fallen into a consumption, and

cannot work any more, and he and his wife and three little children live in one of the rooms over there."

"How do they get along?"

"His wife takes in sewing sometimes, and sometimes goes out washing. Poor Owen! I was over there yesterday; he looks thin and wistful, and his wife was saying that he was parched with constant fever, and had very little appetite. She had, with great self-denial, and by restricting herself almost of necessary food, got him two or three oranges, and the poor fellow seemed so eager after them."

"Poor fellow!" said Eleanor, involuntarily.

"Now, said her aunt, "suppose Owen's wife should get up on Christmas morning, and find at the door a couple of dozen of oranges, and some of those nice white grapes, such as you had at your party last week, don't you think it would make a sensation?"

"Why, yes, I think very likely it might; but who else, aunt? You spoke of a great many."

"Well, on the lower floor there is a neat little room, that is always kept perfectly trim and tidy; it belongs to a young couple who have nothing beyond the husband's day wages to live on. They are, nevertheless, as cheerful and chipper as a couple of wrens, and she is up and down half a dozen times a day, to help poor Mrs. Owen. She has a baby of her own about five months old, and of course does all the cooking, washing, and ironing for herself and husband; and yet, when Mrs. Owen goes out to wash, she takes her baby and keeps it whole days for her."

"I'm sure she deserves that the good fairies should smile on her," said Eleanor; "one baby exhausts my stock of virtue very rapidly."

"But you ought to see her baby," said aunt E., "so plump, so rosy, and good-natured, and always clean as a lily. This baby is a sort of household shrine; nothing is too sacred and too good for it; and I believe the little, thrifty woman feels only one temptation to be extravagant, and that is to get some ornaments to adorn this little divinity."

"Why, did she ever tell you so?'

"No; but one day when I was coming down stairs, the door of their room was partly open, and I saw a pedlar there with open box. John, the husband, was standing with a little purple cap on his hand, which he was regarding with mystified, admiring air, as if he did'nt quite comprehend it, and trim little Mary gazing at it with longing eyes."

"I think we might get it," said John.

"Oh, no," said she, regretfully; "yet I wish we could, it's *so pretty!*"

"Say no more, aunt. I see the good fairy must pop a cap into the window on Christmas morning. Indeed, it shall be done. How they will wonder where it came from, and talk about it for months to come!"

"Well, then," continued her aunt, "in the next street to ours there is a miserable building, that looks as if it were just going to topple over; and away up in the third story, in a little room just under the eaves, live two poor, lonely old women. They are both nearly on to ninety. I was in there day before yesterday. One of them is constantly confined to her bed with rheumatism, the other, weak and feeble, with failing sight and trembling hands, totters about her only helper; and they are entirely dependent on charity."

"Can't they do anything? Can't they knit?" said Eleanor.

"You are young and strong, Eleanor, and have quick eyes and nimble fingers; how long would it take you to knit a pair of stockings?"

"I!" said Eleanor. "What an idea! I never tried, but I think I could get a pair done in a week, perhaps!"

"And if somebody gave you twenty-five cents for them, and out of this you had to get food, and pay room rent, and buy coal for your fire, and oil for your lamp"——

"Stop, aunt, for pity's sake!"

"Well, I will stop, but they can't; they must pay so much every month for that miserable shell they live in, or be turned into the street. The meal and flour that some kind person sends goes off for them just as it does for others, and they must get more or starve, and coal is now scarce and high priced."

"Oh, aunt, I'm quite convinced, I'm sure; don't run me down and annihilate me with all these terrible realities. What shall I do to play a good fairy to these poor old women?"

"If you will give me full power, Eleanor, I will put up a basket to be sent to them, that will give them something to remember all winter."

"Oh, certainly I will. Let me see if I can't think of something myself."

"Well, Eleanor, suppose, then, some fifty, or sixty years hence, if you were old, and your father, and mother, and aunts, and uncles, now so thick around you, laid cold and silent in so many graves—you have somehow got away off to a strange city, where you were never known—you live in a miserable garret, where snow blows at night through the cracks, and the fire is very apt to go out in the old cracked stove; you sit crouching over the dying embers the evening before Christmas—nobody to speak to you, nobody to care for you, except another poor old soul who lies moaning in the bed—now, what would you like to have sent you?"

"Oh, aunt, what a dismal picture!"

"And yet, Ella, all poor, forsaken old women are made of young girls, who expected it in their youth as little as you do, perhaps!"

"Say no more, aunt. I'll buy—let me see—a comfortable warm shawl for each of these poor women; and I'll send them—let me see—oh! some tea—nothing goes down with old women like tea; and I'll make John wheel some coal over to them;

and, aunt, it would not be a very bad thought to send them a new stove. I remember the other day, when mamma was pricing stoves, I saw some, such nice ones, for two or three dollars."

"For a new hand, Ella, you work up the idea very well," said her aunt.

"But how much ought I to give, for any one case, to these women, say?"

"How much did you give last year for any single Christmas present?"

"Why, six or seven dollars, for some; those elegant souvenirs were seven dollars; that ring I gave Mrs. B——— was ten."

"And do you suppose Mrs. B——— was any happier for it?"

"No, really, I don't think she cared much about it; but I had to give her something, because she had sent me something the year before, and I did not want to send a paltry present to any one in her circumstances."

"Then, Ella, give ten to any poor, distressed, suffering creature who really needs it, and see in how many forms of good such a sum will appear. That one hard, cold, glittering diamond ring, that now cheers nobody, and means nothing, that you give because you must, and she takes because she must, might, if broken up into smaller sums, send real warm and heart-felt gladness through many a cold and cheerless dwelling, and through many an aching heart."

"You are getting to be an orator, aunt; but don't you approve of Christmas presents among friends and equals ?"

"Yes, indeed," said her aunt, fondly stroking her head. "I have had some Christmas presents that did me a world of good—a little book mark, for instance, that a certain niece of mine worked for me with wonderful secrecy, three years ago, when she was not a young lady with a purse full of money—that book mark was a true Christmas present; and my young couple across the way are plotting a profound surprise to each other on Christmas morning. John has contrived, by an hour of extra work every night, to lay by enough to get Mary a new calico dress; and she, poor soul, has bargained away the only thing in the jewelry line she ever possessed, to be laid out on a new hat for him."

"I know, too, a washerwoman who has a poor lame boy—a patient, gentle little fellow—who has lain quietly for weeks and months in his little crib, and his mother is going to give him a splendid Christmas present."

" What is it, pray ?"

" A whole orange! Don't laugh. She will pay ten whole cents for it ; for it shall be none of your common oranges, but a picked one of the very best going! She has put by the money, a cent at a time, for a whole month ; and nobody knows which will be happiest in it, Willie or his mother. These are such Christmas presents as I like to think of— gifts coming from love, and tending to produce love ; these are the appropriate gifts of the day.

" But don't you think that it's right for those who *have* money, to give expensive presents, supposing always as you say, they are given from real affection ?"

" Sometimes, undoubtedly. The Saviour did not condemn her who broke an alabaster-box of ointment—*very precious*—simply as a proof of love, even although the suggestion was made, ' this might have been sold for three hundred pence, and given to the poor.' I have thought he would regard with sympathy the fond efforts which human love sometimes makes to express itself by

gifts, the rarest and most costly.   How I rejoiced
with all my heart, when Charles Elton gave his
poor mother that splendid Chinese shawl and gold
watch—because I knew they came from the very
fullness of his heart to a mother that he could not
do too much for—a mother that has done and suffered everything for him.   In some such cases,
when resources are ample, a costly gift seems to
have a graceful appropriateness; but I cannot approve of it, if it exhausts all the means of doing
for the poor; it is better, then, to give a simple
offering, and to do something for those who really
need it."

Eleanor looked thoughtful; her aunt laid down
her knitting, and said, in a tone of gentle serious-
ness:

"Whose birth does Christmas commemorate,
Ella?"

"Our Saviour's, certainly, aunt."

"Yes," said her aunt.   "And when and how
was he born? in a stable! laid in a manger; thus
born, that in all ages he might be known as the
brother and friend of the poor.   And surely it
seems but appropriate to commemorate His birth-
day by an especial remembrance of the lowly,

the poor, the outcast, and distressed; and if Christ should come back to our city on a Christmas day, where should we think it most appropriate to his character to find him? Would he be carrying splendid gifts to splendid dwellings, or would he be gliding about in the cheerless haunts of the desolate, the poor, the forsaken, and the sorrowful?"

And here the conversation ended.

* * * * *

"What sort of Christmas presents is Ella buying?" said cousin Tom, as the waiter handed in a portentous-looking package, which had been just rung in at the door.

"Let's open it," said saucy Will. "Upon my word, two great gray blanket shawls! These must be for you and me, Tom! And what's this? A great bolt of cotton flannel and gray yarn stockings!"

The door bell rang again, and the waiter brought in another bulky parcel, and deposited it on the marble-topped centre table.

"What's here?" said Will, cutting the cord! "Whew! a perfect nest of packages! oolong tea! oranges! grapes! white sugar! Bless me, Ella must be going to housekeeping!"

6

"Or going crazy!" said Tom: "and on my word," said he, looking out of the window, "there's a drayman ringing at our door, with a stove, with a tea-kettle set in the top of it!"

"Ella's cook stove, of course," said Will; and just at this moment the young lady entered, with her purse hanging gracefully over her hand.

"Now, boys, you are too bad!" she exclaimed, as each of the mischievous youngsters were gravely marching up and down, attired in a gray shawl.

"Did'nt you get them for us? We thought you did," said both.

"Ella, I want some of that cotton flannel, to make me a pair of pantaloons," said Tom.

"I say, Ella," said Will, "when are you going to housekeeping? Your cooking stove is standing down in the street; 'pon my word, John is loading some coal on the dray with it."

"Ella, isn't that going to be sent to my office?" said Tom; "do you know I do so languish for a new stove with a tea-kettle in the top, to heat a fellow's shaving water!"

Just then, another ring at the door, and the grinning waiter handed in a small brown paper parcel for Miss Ella. Tom made a dive at it, and staving off the brown paper, developed a jaunty little purple velvet cap, with silver tassels.

"My smoking cap! as I live," said he, "only I shall have to wear it on my thumb, instead of my head—too small entirely," said he, shaking his head gravely.

"Come, you saucy boys," said aunt E——, entering briskly, "what are you teasing Ella for?"

"Why, do see this lot of things, aunt? What in the world is Ella going to do with them?"

"Oh! I know!"

"You know; then I can guess, aunt, it is some of your charitable works. You are going to make a juvenile Lady Bountiful of El, eh?"

Ella, who had colored to the roots of her hair at the expose of her very unfashionable Christmas preparations, now took heart, and bestowed a very gentle and salutary little cuff on the saucy head that still wore the purple cap, and then hastened to gather up her various purchases.

"Laugh away," said she, gaily; "and a good many others will laugh, too, over these things. I got them to make people laugh—people that are not in the habit of laughing!"

"Well, well, I see into it," said Will; "and I

tell you I think right well of the idea, too. There are worlds of money wasted at this time of the year, in getting things that nobody wants, and nobody cares for after they are got; and I am glad, for my part, that you are going to get up a variety in this line; in fact, I should like to give you one of these stray leaves to help on," said he, dropping a $10 note into her paper. I like to encourage girls to think of something besides breastpins and sugar candy."

But our story spins on too long. If anybody wants to see the results of Ella's first attempts at *good fairyism*, they can call at the doors of two or three old buildings on Christmas morning, and they shall hear all about it.